THE WITNESS

After Mitch told his story, he was able to leave the courtroom, and Tucson, if he wished. He didn't want to stick around if he could go back to Paxton, and he already knew the outcome of the trial—they would hang the gang. It was just a matter of when it would happen. There were three circuit hangmen and they were all fairly busy these days.

As Mitch headed out of the courtroom, he passed by Pen, the other Hayes brother. "We'll be seein' you real soon," he whispered. He had a crazed look in his eyes, more so than his brother Elmer. He was long and thin with a narrow face to go with his narrow expression.

Mitch stopped and stared Pen Hayes down. "I don't think you'll get the chance."

"We get out of this, I'm comin' after you, Injun," Pen Hayes said.

"If you get out," Mitch replied, "I'll be waiting."

The *Apache Law* series:
#1: THE LONELY GUN
#2: HELLFIRE
#3: OUTLAW TOWN

Apache Law
Showdown

Luke Adams

LEISURE BOOKS   NEW YORK CITY

A LEISURE BOOK®

October 2000

Published by

Dorchester Publishing Co., Inc.
276 Fifth Avenue
New York, NY 10001

ISBN 0-8439-4786-1

Showdown

Chapter One

The sun had barely peeked over the horizon when Mitch and Alky came in to let the prisoners out of their cells. They'd brought breakfast from Ellie's Eat Here, including hot mugs of strong coffee to burn out any leftover hangover from Saturday night.

The three men in the cells, all miners who had gotten a bit too rowdy on Saturday night and decided to shoot their guns as a way of celebrating finding a particularly large vein of gold, were grateful for both the hot food and the freedom. It would have been a long way back to their claims on empty stomachs.

Abner, the telegraph master, walked into the jailhouse. "Message for you, Sheriff."

Mitch took the paper, thanked Abner, and read it while rolling a smoke. Alky sat nearby, cleaning his shotgun.

"Who's it from?" Alky asked.

"The Tucson sheriff, MacLean." Mitch lit his home-made cigarette and inhaled.

"Must be important if he's sent a telegram here."

Mitch pinched the lit end off of his half-smoked cigarette and put it in his shirt pocket for later. He put the telegram down, got up, and went to the locked gun cabinet. Opening the cabinet, Mitch took his rifle down from the rack and checked his gun to make sure it was loaded. He opened a drawer in his desk and took boxes of bullets out.

All this time, Alky sat and cleaned his gun, occasionally glancing up with open curiosity at Mitch's actions.

"Must be *real* important," Alky finally said.

"Alky, you're in charge."

Alky set his gun aside, stood up, and stretched. "What's goin' on, Mitch?"

"Pen and Elmer Hayes and their gang just stuck up a bank in Tucson. Killed everyone in the building and got clean away."

"Goddamn. The Hayes gang," Alky said. "They're a dangerous bunch." He started to gather up his own rifle and gun. "I better go with you."

Mitch shook his head. "Someone needs to keep an eye on our town. They're headed north, according to Sheriff MacLean. If they get past me, I want you here to protect the town. I'm gonna try to meet up with the posse."

Alky grumbled about it, but Mitch knew that his deputy saw the sense in it. The law couldn't just go off and leave Paxton unprotected.

"Want me to tell Mr. Reid where you went?" Alky asked.

8

Mitch paused. "I'd better go see him myself. We got something to discuss anyways."

J. Paxton Reid, founder and mayor of Paxton, was in his office. Through the open door, Mitch could see that Reid was with Bill Carson, manager of the mine. Jewel Reid, the mayor's daughter, was entering numbers in a ledger. She looked up and when she saw it was Mitch, she smiled.

"You want me to tell my father you're here?" she asked.

He nodded toward Reid and Carson, who were just coming out of the office. Reid was both mayor and founder of Paxton. He was slightly overweight, red-faced, and balding.

"Sheriff," Carson greeted Mitch as he passed by.

"Come on in," Reid said to Mitch. He closed the office door.

Inside, Mitch handed the telegram to Reid, who read it silently. He looked up. "Don't you think you'd better go down there?"

"I was planning to, but I thought I'd better let you know first."

Reid raised his eyebrows. "You're the law. I didn't think you'd need my approval for this."

The resentment that had been suppressed for so long in Mitch finally surfaced. "You're the one holding a false signed confession to murder over my head."

Reid's eyes widened. "Don't you have a job that you're good at? Don't you have friends here now? Aren't you settled in yet? Hell, the way I see it, I gave you a life."

Mitch ran a hand through his black hair before saying something. "You don't see anything wrong with keeping me here against my will, do you? I'm a prisoner here, same as the men I hold in the cells on the weekends."

Reid walked around to the other side of his desk. "Let me ask you something. If I took that confession out and burned it in front of you, would you stay here of your own free will and remain sheriff of this town?"

Mitch thought about it. "I can't give you an answer. I don't know."

Reid shook his head. "Then I can't take the chance of giving up a damn good sheriff, no matter how I got you." He took a cigar out of the box on the corner of his desk, then offered one to Mitch, who shook his head. Reid took a small knife and cut the end off, then lit it. "Of course you have to go help Sheriff MacLean. If some outlaws stuck up our bank, I would expect the same courtesy." He looked up at Mitch. "Just don't be gone too long."

"Alky's in charge while I'm gone." He turned quickly and left the office before he gave in to his impulse to punch Reid in the face.

Mitch left the outer office with a curt nod to Jewel. She must have heard the raised voices in the office because Mitch noticed that she looked concerned.

Within fifteen minutes, Mitch had checked his gear and supplies and was headed out of Paxton south toward Tucson. It was a blue-sky day with a few wispy clouds scudding across the sky. Mitch shouldn't have had a care in the world.

Instead, he thought about what had happened, how he had ended up in Paxton, as sheriff of a boomtown. There were good things about it, he reminded himself. He got paid real well, better than most jobs, and the work was sometimes interesting. Now was such a time. Heading south to meet up with Sheriff MacLean's posse and tracking the outlaws was going to exercise the skills he'd learned from the years he spent as a civilian scout for the Army.

He met up with the posse in midafternoon. There were five men with MacLean. The sheriff was a tall, lean, older man with a salt-and-pepper mustache and bushy eyebrows. He brought Mitch up to date on what he knew about the robbery.

"Elmer and Pen Hayes were in Yuma a few years ago for robbing a stagecoach. That's where they met up with Rolly and Lefty. They got out about four years ago, and were quiet for a time, but recently, there's been a spate of bank robberies in this territory."

"They hadn't killed anyone before this?" Mitch asked, his eyes on the tracks left by the gang members.

"Nope," MacLean replied. "Not that we ever knew about. None of 'em. I think one of the bank clerks or a customer must have tried to get to his gun, but no witnesses were left alive to tell us how it happened."

"So we're looking for four gang men?"

Sheriff MacLean scratched his beard. "Well, now, that's an interesting question. There were four gang members who left the scene of the Tucson State Bank massacre, but I read the wanted posters, and it mentions five gang members the last time the gang struck a bank up near Colorado about two years ago. But the citizens who witnessed the gang leave the bank swear there were only four of 'em."

"Did anyone see the gang ride out of town?"

"I have a deputy asking questions. He found someone who swears he saw five men riding out of town."

Mitch thought about it. "They have the names?"

The sheriff shook his head. "Got four names for you: Pen and Elmer Hayes, George 'Lefty' Forbes and John 'Rolly' Rollins. Fifth man couldn't be identified."

"Could be the witness was mistaken."

"Could be. Might not be able to count." MacLean took off his hat and wiped the sweat off his forehead. "You used to scout for the Army, didn't you?"

"Rode with Al Sieber and Tom Horn."

"Good men. Sorry to see the Army cut all of you loose. But Mr. Reid is real happy you decided to stay on in Paxton."

"I bet he is," was all Mitch could say. He changed the subject. "We've been following riderless horses."

"Why do you say that?"

Mitch had been following the track from atop his horse and was irritated with himself for not noticing the track patterns sooner. He got down and examined the depth of the prints closely. "The hoof marks are too shallow to be horses with riders. Also, horses without riders tend to run in more of a zigzag pattern with one horse leading the rest. These tracks suggest that. If there were riders, the pattern would be different."

The sheriff wheeled his horse around. "The gang probably had a second set of horses waiting somewhere between where we met up and here. They changed horses and sent these riderless ones this way while they forded the river."

Mitch pulled his makings out of his saddlebag and rolled a cigarette. He got back on his horse, lit up, and smoked it while he thought. "What's the closest point to the river between here and Tucson?"

The sheriff thought a moment. "A couple of miles

back, we were about half a mile from the river."

MacLean decided that several of his men would go on ahead, just to be sure they didn't miss anything. At the least, they would be able to gather up the horses while the other half of the posse followed Mitch and the sheriff.

Mitch got off his horse when they got to the spot. He walked around, and about a quarter mile away, he found the hoofprints of the waiting horses, near a small scrubby tree. MacLean came over. "Looks like you were right."

Mitch shrugged and rolled a cigarette. "Just made sense to me. I put myself in the position of the hunted—what would I do?"

They followed a new set of tracks until they stopped at the riverbank. MacLean wanted to cross.

"The Hayes gang might have walked their horses down river—there's enough brush around here to hide them from sight and if they stayed in the water, they wouldn't leave a trail." Mitch stayed on one side of the river and the sheriff rode on the other side, both men scanning the horizon for signs of the gang. Mitch stopped his horse and squinted to the northeast. "There they are." He pointed to four figures about a mile away on the flat desert horizon.

The posse rode hard and long to catch up to the killers. There was no point in trying to be stealthy. It was better to let the gang know the posse was on to them at this point. They would make mistakes while scrambling for a way to escape. One man was captured early on when his horse stumbled and broke its leg. The other three men left him behind without looking back.

As the posse approached the injured man, the sheriff drew his gun. The painful grunts of the horse could be heard by all. The other horses danced nervously around, sensing that one of their own was in agony.

"Keep an eye on him, Joe," MacLean ordered one of his men.

"We'll be here," Joe said, drawing his gun and training it on the injured man.

As the posse continued on, Mitch turned to MacLean. "I'll be along." He went back, took his rifle out, nodded to Joe, and shot the animal with the broken leg to put it out of its misery.

When Mitch caught up with the posse, MacLean asked, "Which animal did you kill?"

"Not the one you're thinking about. That was a waste of a good horse."

A few hours later, the posse caught up to the gang as they neared the mountains. The remaining three members of the gang dashed over to a couple of boulders while shooting at the posse. One of the sheriff's men was shot before reaching the safety of a saguaro cactus.

MacLean tried to drag the body with him. Shots rang out, a bullet chipping the cactus. Cactus juice leaked from the saguaro.

"Leave him," Mitch called out.

"We might be able to save him," the sheriff said. A shot grazed the sheriff's arm. Mitch turned to the man next to him, a fellow whose name he didn't even know.

"You and the others cover me while I help the sheriff."

The other man nodded and began firing in earnest.

Mitch ran a zigzag pattern to help MacLean drag his man to safety.

When they got back to their shelter, MacLean nodded his thanks.

"I've been thinking," Mitch said. "Can you and the men distract them with a volley of fire? Just keep it up so they won't be able to look over the boulders without getting shot at."

MacLean nodded and instructed his men. Mitch waited until the firing began and, ducking low and to the right, sprinted for the cover of a boulder he'd spotted earlier. From there, he was able to circle around and climb up until he was above the three men. They had started shooting again, and this was when Mitch made his move. When he looked over the cliff of his vantage point, one of the men was loading a gun. He looked up and saw Mitch, yelled to his compatriots, and they turned on Mitch. But it was too late. Mitch covered the three outlaws with his Navy Colt.

"If you want to stay alive, drop your guns."

One of the men got off a shot and Mitch dropped him with a shot to the forehead. The other two men looked at each other and dropped their guns.

Calling to the sheriff, Mitch marched the two remaining gang members out into the open. While two of the sheriff's men handcuffed the gang members, Mitch collected the guns and the rifle.

Sheriff MacLean looked over to Mitch before they got back on their horses. "Nice work. Thanks."

They picked up the other gang member and guard on their way back, and the sheriff sent one of his men off to catch up to the other half of the posse that had followed the false trail.

When they reached the point where Paxton branched off from Tucson, Mitch bid good-bye to the sheriff and headed north. As Mitch passed the injured gang member, the man gave him a dirty look. Mitch met the outlaw's eyes with an even look. The other members of the gang, Rolly Rollins and Pen Hayes, sat sullenly on their horses. Lefty Forbes's body was strapped over his horse.

Mitch parted ways with no more than a nod to Sheriff MacLean.

A week later, he got a message from MacLean requesting his presence at the Hayes gang's trial. Alky deputized a couple of men, Sam Neely and Ollie Burns, so Mitch could ride down to Tucson.

Mitch didn't like Tucson mostly because it was too big for his taste. A lot of people didn't like Indians, Apaches especially, and with Mitch's mixed blood, he could walk into a town like Tucson and be challenged to a fight without any provocation other than being a half-breed.

Even when he was cut loose from the Army and rode for a few days with Tom Horn and Al Sieber, he parted ways with them before they got to Tucson. Al and Tom didn't care that Mitch's father was an Apache.

But coming into Tucson this time wasn't so bad—he knew where he had to be, and he didn't intend to stay any longer than was necessary. J. Paxton Reid had read the message from MacLean, and encouraged Mitch to go.

"Think of it as a well-deserved holiday," he'd said. Reid even tried to give Mitch some money for a hotel and food.

Mitch turned him down. "I won't be there long enough to need a bed for the night." He left early the next morning and got there an hour before the trial. MacLean met him outside the courtroom, which had just been built.

"Good to see you again, Sheriff," MacLean greeted him. "We have time for a drink."

"Coffee, if you don't mind," Mitch said.

The sheriff indicated a little café across the street and they sat at a table. A man brought them steaming mugs of strong coffee.

"If you can't drink it," he said, "you can always use it to tan buffalo hides."

Mitch and the sheriff chuckled as the man left.

"How've the boys been behavin'?" Mitch asked.

"Ornery. They been hollerin' a lot about their rights. I keep sayin' we'll go easy on the one who turns in the money."

"The money's still missing?"

MacLean nodded. "Seems they hid it sometime during their run."

The two lawmen finished up their coffee and headed over to the courthouse.

When Mitch was called to tell what he knew, all three outlaws' mouths were set in mean lines.

As Mitch passed, Elmer Hayes hissed, "Injun!" and spat at him. Elmer had badly pitted ruddy skin and was missing a tooth in front.

The sheriff nodded to a deputy near Elmer and the deputy leaned over and backhanded the prisoner across the mouth. The judge ignored what was happening and called to the lawyer to get on with it.

MacLean strode across the room and leaned into El-

17

mer Hayes. "He's a better man than you are any day,
half-breed or not, so shut your trap."

After Mitch told his story, he was able to leave the
courtroom, and Tucson, if he wished. He didn't want
to stick around if he could go back to Paxton, and he
already knew the outcome of the trial—they would
hang the gang. It was just a matter of when it would
happen. There were three circuit hangmen and they
were all fairly busy these days.

As Mitch headed out of the courtroom, he passed by
Pen, the other Hayes brother. "We'll be seein' you real
soon," he whispered. He had a crazed look in his eyes,
more so than his brother Elmer. He was long and thin
with a narrow face to go with his narrow expression.

Mitch stopped and stared Pen Hayes down. "I don't
think you'll get the chance."

"We get out of this, I'm comin' after you, Injun,"
Pen Hayes said.

"If you get out," Mitch replied, "I'll be waiting."

Chapter Two

Mitch Frye rolled a cigarette from his makings and tipped his chair back at his desk. Except for the regulars who got drunk on Saturday night and shot up the town, things had been a little quiet in Paxton. Any other sheriff might have not minded being in charge of a quiet town, but Mitch was different. He was restless when it was too quiet. And it was only Monday. A long way from Friday.

When Mitch was cut loose from his scout job with the Army, along with his friends Tom Horn and Al Sieber, he hadn't had time to figure out what he wanted to do. He drifted into Paxton to get the reward on two killers who'd tried to get the drop on him. Before he knew it, he had been tricked into accepting the position of sheriff of Paxton.

Mitch still had a sore spot in him because of the way Reid held a so-called signed confession over him for killing a man Reid had contracted him to go after and

19

bring back. It wasn't as though Dunklee, the man who had stolen Reid's money and possibly killed another employee of Reid's, had given Mitch a choice in the matter. When a man shot at Mitch, he figured there was an intent to kill and he was obliged to shoot back. And he shot to kill, too.

But lately, he'd been pretty settled in the job, making a few good friends and making more money than he had ever had as a civilian scout with the Army. It chapped him every once in a while to know that Reid was still holding the signed confession. But Mitch had to admit that he was pretty good at his job and the likelihood of Reid ever using that piece of paper he held was becoming less of a reality every day. And the likelihood of Mitch ever leaving his job of sheriff in any way other than a pine box seemed even more remote.

Being a half-breed, Mitch had felt out of place all his life. He never knew his Apache father, and although his white mother had raised him and loved him, other white folks didn't want anything to do with him. So he'd grown up mostly by himself.

He finished his smoke, got up and stretched, then thought he might walk around the town to make his presence known before Friday night arrived. He wanted the rowdies to remember that he was here.

As he stepped out of his office, he caught sight of Reid getting off his horse near Ellie's Eat Here tent café. Reid saw him and nodded and Mitch returned the nod.

He was never able to be completely friendly with the man because of their shared past. To add to that, Reid's lovely, headstrong daughter, Jewel, had an in-

terest in Mitch, and Reid didn't approve of their friendship. He made it known every chance he got, but Jewel
was determined to lead her own life, and if she wanted
to talk to Mitch, she was damned if her father was
going to tell her whom she could be friends with.

At first, Mitch had taken every opportunity to be
with Jewel just to make Reid uncomfortable, on the off
chance that the mayor would let Mitch out of his contract to protect his daughter's honor. But over time,
Mitch had found Jewel to be a good person to talk with.
She was one of the few people in town that he considered to be a good friend.

When he first arrived in Paxton and had been on the
job for less than a week, some people weren't happy
about having a half-Apache for a sheriff. A couple of
them met him on a road outside of town and beat him
up so bad he almost didn't make it back to town. Mitch
was too beat up to take care of himself. Between Jewel
and the town doctor, they got him back on his feet.
Jewel was also a good listener, often making him rethink a case he might be working on. She had a good
mind. She was also very pretty.

Mitch passed the newspaper building where Harvey
Radin worked. Harvey had come to town just after
Mitch and had started a damn fine paper. Harvey
wasn't in the front office, which probably meant he was
setting the type in the back.

The assay office had a few customers. Mondays were
never very busy. But it brought to mind Mitch's deputy, Alky, who had just bought a small claim close to
town. When Alky wasn't working as deputy sheriff on
the weekends, he was working the stake he'd bought
from a greenhorn who'd had gold dust in his eyes when

he'd come to Paxton. The greenhorn didn't last out three months, and Alky was now realizing his dream of mining gold when he wasn't helping Mitch round up the drunks and troublemakers on the weekends.

A horse and rider came fast down Main Street and stopped outside Mitch's office. "Sheriff!" The rider hopped off and ran up to Mitch. It was Manny, one of the miners. "Sheriff! Alky's broke his leg or somethin'. He's complainin' of a pain in his leg."

"Where is he?" Mitch asked, knowing full well where Alky was. But it was a way to keep Manny talking while he thought some.

"He's out at his claim. I stopped by his shack to borrow some coffee. I found him passed out at the bottom of a ravine. I left a bottle of whiskey for him and came directly into town."

"Thanks, Manny." Mitch grabbed his hat and strode over to the stable, telling Sam Neely to get his horse ready. He turned back to Manny. "Get the doc. Tell him to meet me over at the claim. I'll ride out there to stay with Alky till Doc arrives."

It didn't take long to ride to Alky's claim. It was on the edge of Paxton on a small creek. Mitch hoped Alky hadn't broken his leg. That would take a long time to heal and right now, he couldn't think of one man in town he'd want to have as a deputy while Alky was healing.

When Mitch got to the mining shack, he spied Alky's gray horse tethered outside the makeshift shack. The greenhorn—no one ever knew his name because he didn't stay long enough—had been a carpenter by trade and his shack was a testament to his abilities. Solidly built with a bed, a table, and a small stove for cooking inside, it was practically a castle compared to most miners' shacks. Reid had tried to get the man to stay on as a carpenter, since they'd lost one of their carpenters due to his being a killer, but the greenhorn was bound and determined to try his luck at silver mining up in Nevada Territory.

"Alky!" Mitch called out. He heard groaning and followed the sound till he found Alky at the bottom of a deep ravine. Alky lay like a downed buffalo. The bottle next to him was empty.

"Damn!" Mitch muttered. "Not only hurt, but drunk now." Silently cursing Manny for his good intentions gone bad, Mitch climbed down the ravine to get a better look at Alky's injuries. He was singing to himself at this point.

"Buffalo gals, won't you come out tonight, come out tonight, come out t'night—" Alky looked up, his eyes out of focus. "Hey, Sheriff. Whatcha doin' out here? Need me to come roust some drunksh—" He tried to get up, but failed miserably. "Ooopsh." He grinned at Mitch.

"Have you tried to stand on it?" Mitch asked.

"Yup. Fell down again. Damn, it hurt. But not no more. I can try again." Alky started to get up, Mitch getting an arm around his deputy's waist. "Aaaagh!" He sat down again. "Hell!"

Mitch rolled Alky's pants leg up his left leg and saw the ankle, already turning purple and swollen. Mitch unlaced Alky's boot. "Looks sprained to me, but it's a bad one."

He heard the sound of Doc's buggy and Manny's horse and climbed out of the ditch. After greeting them, Mitch gave them an assessment of Alky's situation.

23

While Doc attended to his passed-out patient, Manny and Mitch gathered enough sturdy branches to make a travois. Manny found rope in Alky's shack and they lashed the branches together until the travois was strong enough to hold Alky's weight. At least, they hoped so. Mitch climbed into the ravine with Alky and the doc, and Manny lowered the makeshift transport to the two able-bodied men.

Doc Henshaw was a young fellow, also a failed miner, who decided to go back to his more honest profession of healing. Miners often had ailments and injuries, and Doc Henshaw was pretty good at relieving most any complaint a body had. Together, Doc and Mitch rolled Alky's inert form onto the travois.

"I'm a-tyin' the ropes to my horse, Sheriff," Manny called down to them. "Give me the signal and I'll pull the horse forward."

"I'll leave you to supervise, Doc." With some difficulty, Mitch climbed back out and helped guide the horse straight.

Once Alky was loaded onto Doc's buggy, they all headed back for town. At the doc's surgery, Alky was checked and pronounced fine except for a badly sprained ankle. "Have him stay off it for a couple of days," Doc Henshaw told Mitch. "Then he can use this crutch to get around for the next few weeks." He handed a crudely carved crutch to Mitch. Alky was awake by now. They loaded him in Doc's buggy again and got him over to his place in town, the new hotel that went up a few months ago, and got him settled in.

"Damn," Alky grumbled, still woozy from the whiskey, "can't b'lieve I slipped down that big hole. Whatcha gonna do, Sheriff, without me by your side for a few days?"

Mitch scratched his head. "I'll manage. It's been quiet around here."

Alky screwed up his face in thought. "Maybe a little too quiet."

"What do you mean?"

"You know how it goes—everything's goin' fine, but somethin' like this happens and suddenly you'll find out how much you need me around."

Mitch almost smiled. "I gotta tell Ellie to come around and feed you."

"Yeah, and I could use some sportin' while I'm down. Tell Fanny Belle she can send a girl over here in a day or two. Think Reid'll pay for that?" he asked with a wry grin.

Mitch smiled. "Sounds like you're better already."

"A little sportin' and I'll be right as rain." Alky suddenly looked tired. He slumped down in his bed and closed his eyes. "Gotta get me some rest."

A moment later, Alky was snoring. Mitch left his room and headed back to his office.

Chapter Three

Mitch went over to Ellie's Eat Here tent café and told her about Alky. She'd already heard about it from Manny, who'd come in for some grub and coffee.

"I'll make sure Alky's taken care of," she told Mitch with a wink. "You want some peach pie? I got some canned peaches in the other day and baked some peach pie."

Mitch sat down and a minute later, Ellie sat a big wedge of pie in front of him and filled a mug with coffee. J. Paxton Reid came in when Mitch was half-way through the pie. He sat down opposite Mitch and signaled Ellie for coffee. She brought him the same as Mitch.

"Damn, peach pie! Miss Ellie, I think I'd better make an honest woman out of you," Reid said.

Ellie looked mock angry. "What do you mean, make an honest woman of me? If I wasn't, I'd be down at Fanny Belle's right now and you wouldn't have any peach pie in front of you." Ellie moved away to serve some other customers who'd just sat down. Reid chuckled. "So, Mitch, I hear Alky got himself into a little trouble out at his claim."

"Manny told you?"

"Hell, with Manny, it's all over town five minutes after it's news," Reid replied.

Mitch nodded. Ellie came back to fill up his mug with more coffee.

"You need a new deputy or what?"

"I might ask around to fill Alky's shoes till his ankle's better," Mitch said.

"How 'bout Manny?"

Mitch grimaced. "He's too much at his site. Not a miner. Can't think of anyone right yet. I'll be all right for a while."

"When Friday night comes, you're gonna have your hands full when the miners turn loose in this town," Reid pointed out. He polished his plate, practically licking it clean, then pushed back and pulled a cigar out. Mitch rolled a cigarette and lit it. They puffed in silence for a while.

Down the street, some shooting started up. Mitch threw his cigarette down and crushed it out with his boot heel. He got up and touched his six-gun just to make sure. "Duty calls," he said, touched his hat, then headed for the saloon.

It was the Bad Dog again. When Red Calhoun first came to town, he'd set up the saloon and gambling establishment right away. A former gambler himself, he was now content to fleece the general public of their money and nuggets at the gambling tables and the bar. Calhoun had just put a fresh coat of green paint on the saloon building. As Mitch approached, he could still smell the paint fumes.

A scrawny whiskered man staggered out into the street, clutching his arm. Another man strode out of the Bad Dog, Navy Colt drawn and ready to shoot. The second man wasn't from Paxton, but he looked familiar to Mitch.

Mitch unholstered his own gun and pointed it at the man with the drawn gun.

"What's the trouble here?" he called out.

The injured man loped toward him. Blood was seeping out from between his fingers where he'd been shot. Mitch recognized him as one of the men who worked for Reid's mining operation and had a claim on the side. He didn't know the man well, but he conjured up a first name, Alvin, and he seemed to recall his impression of Alvin as sly.

"Sheriff, this stranger says I cheated at cards. It was a fair game. He just lost. I had a flush and he had a straight. Flush beats a straight any day." Alvin set his jaw.

"Go get yourself seen by Doc Henshaw," Mitch told him. "I'll take care of this."

The other man was hard-eyed and stone-faced. He had long dark brown hair tied back and wore a faded blue shirt and denims. He looked as if he'd just gotten to town—he hadn't shaved for a few days and his clothes still had dust from the road on them. That feeling that he was familiar to Mitch came up again.

The man hesitated, eyeing Mitch's badge, then holstered his gun. Mitch noticed that the man wore his belt low slung—he'd seen guns worn this way mostly on guns for hire. Made it easier to get at the gun in a pinch. An extra second to draw could be the difference between life and death.

"What's the problem?"

The man nodded to him. "Sheriff. Man there wasn't telling the entire truth. I caught him dealing from the bottom of the deck. We all saw the bottom card before he put the deck down the first time. Man to his right tapped the cards instead of cutting them. It was draw poker and he dealt me a card from the top, dealt the others their cards, and then discarded one card for himself. Funny thing is, the flush he laid down included the jack of clubs that we'd seen earlier at the bottom of the deck."

A couple more men came out, clearly the other players. Homer, the owner of the general store, was one of them. So was Herman Connelly, a miner, and Ollie Burns, who worked construction whenever he wasn't mining. In fact, Ollie was the one who painted the Bad Dog. Red came out, too. He was a burly man with red hair and a florid face. His sleeves were rolled up, revealing strong arms and thick wrists.

The stranger continued. "These men are my witnesses. I called him on the deal and he called me a liar. Made as if to draw, and I got to my gun first."

Red nodded to Mitch. "Sheriff."

Mitch turned to Red. "Had a little trouble here, did you? Can you tell me what you know about this, Red?"

Red nodded in the direction of the injured miner, who was fast making a retreat. "Alvin's always been a little mean. I caught the move. He dealt a card to himself from the bottom of the deck."

Ollie and Homer agreed with Red.

"I seen him slip the card from the deck. He was lookin' real sly," Ollie said.

Homer added, "Alvin'd been losing a lot of his poke, and I think he wanted to get a little back. He shouldn't't've lied, though, when this gentleman caught him cheating. We all saw the card; you'd have to be blind, deaf, and dumb not to have seen that bottom card."

Herman admitted he didn't see anything. "Guess I wasn't paying too much attention," he said, rubbing the back of his neck. "I folded early anyway. I had nothing for a hand."

Mitch let everyone go but the stranger. When the others had gone back inside the Bad Dog for a drink, Mitch turned back to the stranger. "When'd you get into town?"

The man grinned. He was handsome in a sly way. "Just this morning. Had a long, hard ride from Colorado. How'd you know I just got in?"

"It's my business to know," Mitch said. "How about telling me your name." Not that it would do Mitch any good when he went back to the office to look through wanted posters—half the men in town had changed their names when they came West. Most men were running from something more than they were running to anything.

The man hesitated for a fraction of a second. "Beaumont. Trace Beaumont," he finally said.

"Well, Trace, my name's Sheriff Frye. Mitch Frye." He stuck out his hand. Beaumont grabbed it and pumped.

"Well, well, little Mitch, sheriff of this place. How the hell are you?"

Mitch grinned. "Good. You?"

"Shaking the dust off the trail," Beaumont replied. "Hell, how many years has it been?"

Mitch shook his head. "Can't count that high. Where you stayin'?"

"That hotel over there." Beaumont indicated the Gold Dust Hotel, one of the fancier hotels in town.

Mitch raised his eyebrows. "You must be doing well."

Beaumont shrugged.

"Mitch," a feminine voice called.

He looked around to see Jewel Reid coming toward him. She was a pretty thing, that was for sure. And she had a mind of her own, more than he could say for most women these days.

"Jewel. You're out of work early."

She glanced at Beaumont before replying. "When your employer is your father, sometimes you can get out a little early. Actually, I came over to get some supplies for the mine."

"Miss Reid, this is Trace Beaumont, an old friend. Trace, this is Miss Jewel Reid. Her daddy started this town and is mayor. He also owns the biggest mine in Paxton."

Beaumont stepped forward and took one of Jewel's hands, bending over it in the old-fashioned greeting. It bothered Mitch a little, but he couldn't say for sure why. He didn't own Jewel, but the way Beaumont looked at her was the way a starving man eyed a rare steak. "Miss Reid, I am mighty glad to meet you."

Jewel gave Beaumont the smile Mitch usually saw her reserve for times when she wasn't sure what to think. He was glad of her reaction. She was a girl with

31

sense and didn't let fancy words or actions turn her head.

Withdrawing her hand from his as soon as she possibly could, she asked, "What brings you to Paxton, Mr. Beaumont?"

"I was just riding through with a couple of companions. On my way to Tucson. But I like this town. I might stay a few days."

Jewel was beginning to edge out of their conversation. "Well, good day, Mr. Beaumont." Before she left, she turned to Mitch. "I almost forgot what I came over to tell you. Just wanted to remind you about the social coming up next Sunday. I've been asked to contribute a box and wanted to make sure someone would buy it."

Mitch wasn't much for socializing, but ever since the Reverend Mr. Wesslund, the local circuit preacher, had included Paxton on his route, the Paxton population had been getting a Baptist sermon once every couple of weeks. And the good Reverend Mr. Wesslund wouldn't let Mitch get away with sleeping in on the Sundays he appeared.

One day he came calling on Mitch to introduce himself. "I would be much obliged if you would attend my services, Sheriff. Sometimes when the Holy Spirit fills a body, a person can get a mite possessed."

Mitch took it to mean that because the preacher's Sunday service was held at the Golden Monkey Saloon, he wanted to make sure that everyone got a dose of religion and not a dose of whiskey. He'd been attending the preacher's services since then. The social was the first to be held since Wesslund started coming through.

Mitch nodded to Jewel. "I'll be there."

Beaumont stepped up next to Mitch. "As will I. I'm sure you are a fine cook, Miss Reid."

Mitch looked over at Beaumont. It was hard to believe that he was seeing Trace Beaumont again. When they were growing up together, Trace had been the only boy who didn't seem to mind Mitch's company. Mitch wouldn't go so far as to say that they had been friends, but he owed a debt to Trace, and he would be hospitable, even though something about Trace troubled him.

Trace turned to Mitch. "So, Sheriff, what do you plan to do about the situation in the Bad Dog?"

Mitch shook his head. "I'll go see about Alvin's shoulder and find out what he wants to do about the shooting. Don't leave town without talking to me first. I know where you're staying, so I'll get back to you."

As Mitch turned to leave, Trace called out, "Is there any good place to eat around here? I was planning on having an early dinner. Care to join me? We can talk over old times."

Mitch stopped and thought about it. He wasn't feeling particularly nostalgic, but he did owe Trace for saving his life that one time. And he was curious about what Trace had been up to lately. Mitch had a feeling that there was more to Trace—he got the feeling that Trace wasn't just passing through town. He wanted to know more about him.

"Ellie's Eat Here café," Mitch said. "I'll meet you there for dinner."

When Mitch got to the doc's surgery, Alvin was being patched up.

"Just a graze," Doc Henshaw told Mitch. "He'll live."

"What's your version of how you got shot, Alvin?"

Alvin had had some time to think about it and probably realized that his clumsy and desperate attempt to cheat his way to a winning hand was doomed. He looked somewhat embarrassed. "Guess I was caught cheatin'."

"Is there anything else you'd like to tell me?" Mitch asked.

Alvin opened his mouth, then shut it and shook his head.

"You want to press charges?"

Alvin shook his head a second time. "I got carried away, I guess. Had a good week down at the claim, came into town to celebrate, and ended up losing most of my poke to that card sharp. My fault." He looked sad.

"You know anything more about the man who shot you?" Mitch noted a fresh bruise on Alvin's cheek that he didn't remember seeing when he encountered Alvin earlier.

Alvin opened his mouth as if he was going to say something, then closed it and shook his head. "Never seen him before he walked into the Bad Dog and asked if he could join us for a game of cards."

"How was he doing at cards before he shot you?"

Alvin shrugged. "Okay, I guess. He won a couple of hands. He wasn't cheatin', if that's what you're gettin' at."

Mitch nodded. "I'll walk you out, Alvin."

When they got outside, Mitch rolled a cigarette and smoked it. "You gonna be all right? Can I spot you

34

some money?" Mitch knew Alvin wasn't the sort of man who normally gambled his money away. But he'd always thought Alvin was a man who could easily get in trouble for making the wrong decision. Today was a perfect example. He almost got himself killed cheating at cards.

"Nah, but thanks, Sheriff. I'm paid up on my diggings and I get good lay from Mr. Reid. I'm set for a time." Alvin shook his head sorrowfully. "Thought I'd be able to spend a few dollars and have a little fun. Just don't have nothing extra for drink or cards now."

"If you've a mind, there's a social on Sunday after the reverend saves a few souls. You can spend time at the Bad Dog without losing anything but a little time."

Alvin screwed his face up in distaste. "Ain't the same. Jesus in a saloon. I'll wait till I get my lay from Mr. Reid."

"You'll miss the social," Mitch called after him.

Alvin waved at him as he headed home, a room in the cheapest hotel in town.

Mitch went back to his office and checked his wanted posters. They were badly out of date. He ended up putting half of them aside because he knew or suspected that some of the outlaws were caught or dead. He would sort through them later.

He couldn't find a wanted poster on Trace Beaumont, but he bet that there was a price on Trace's head somewhere. A man didn't wear his holster low slung like that and not have a well-deserved reputation. And maybe Trace was justified to shoot at Alvin, but another man would have let it go and left the table, maybe gone to the law to deal with the cheater. Only a gunslinger would act the way Trace did with no remorse for shooting a man.

On his way to find Trace again, Mitch detoured to the general store where a telegraph was set up. There was talk of the railroad coming in, and Mitch knew that Reid was involved in the negotiations. If that happened, the telegraph would probably move out there.

He gave Abner a message to send to the Tucson sheriff, asking about any wanted posters on a Trace Beaumont. After he paid for the message, he went looking for Trace again.

Mitch found Trace drinking at the Bad Dog. Trace gestured to him to come over, then told Red to get Mitch a drink.

"I usually don't drink this early in the day," Mitch said.

"Special occasion," Trace said. "The meeting of two old friends."

Mitch didn't really think of Trace as a friend, but he didn't object.

"Did you ever learn to swim?" Trace asked.

"Years later."

When Mitch was seven, he'd gotten a cramp while swimming in the local water hole. Problem was that he was out in the deepest part of the water hole and there was no one around to help him. He was barely keeping his head above water when Trace came along. They'd never been friends, but Trace had never bothered Mitch the way the other kids did. Without even thinking about it, Trace dove in and dragged Mitch to dry land.

They never became fast friends. Trace hardly acknowledged Mitch before or after that, but Mitch always felt beholden to Trace. Now Trace was acting as if they were long-lost buddies. Mitch felt that time could change a man for the better or for the worse. He hadn't made up his mind about Trace yet.

Trace shook his head. "Any time I hear someone saying that Indians can swim, I tell 'em about you and how I saved you."

"I'm only half Apache," Mitch reminded him mildly. He was irritated that Trace would bring it up. Mitch didn't like anyone making assumptions that because he had some Indian in him, he should swim better or drink more or creep more silently through the woods, or even track better than other men. Tom Horn and Al Sieber didn't have a drop of Indian blood in them and Mitch considered them to be two of the finest scouts he'd ever worked with.

"Yeah, you're a half-breed." Trace must have seen the look on Mitch's face, because he quickly added, "No offense meant. It's a description, not an insult."

"Some people mean it as an insult," Mitch said. "Apology accepted."

"So, how long you been sheriff?"

" 'Bout a year."

"What were you doin' before that?"

"Scoutin' for the Army."

"No kidding?" Trace asked. "With who?"

Mitch looked at him. "You ask an awful lot of questions."

Trace grinned. "We got a lot of catching up to do. You work for Crook?"

"Yeah."

"Then you know Tom Horn and Al Sieber."

"I knew 'em," Mitch allowed, not adding that he considered Tom and Al two of the best friends he'd ever had. He'd felt as if he belonged with them. They didn't care about a man's past as long as he did his job.

"I ran into Horn up in Colorado not too long ago. He was wearing a badge," Trace said as he finished his drink and signaled to Red for another.

"You remember what town?" Mitch was interested. In case he ever got out of Paxton without a price on his head, he might look Horn up.

Trace seemed to think on it, then shook his head. "Nah. I was just passing through."

Mitch was glad to hear that Tom Horn was doing well. He wondered about Al Sieber, where he was and what he decided to do after the Army cut them all loose.

It was getting to be suppertime.

Trace must have read his mind. "You want to go over to that place you mentioned and get some grub?"

They left the saloon. As they stepped outside, a younger man passed them on his way in. He also had the look of a gunslinger. He looked at Trace as if he was going to say something to him, then thought better of it. Trace didn't react, but it bothered Mitch. It looked to him as if the other man knew Trace, but something stopped him from talking to Trace. Mitch wondered if it was the company that he was keeping.

"You know him?" Mitch asked. "He looked like he wanted to say something to you."

"I rode into town with him," Trace replied. Mitch felt there was more to his answer, but he didn't press the issue.

Ellie's special was buffalo steak. Both men ordered it. Boiled, mashed carrots and turnips and freshly baked bread accompanied the steak when Ellie set a plate in front of each of them.

"So, tell me what you've been doing," Mitch said.

"I did a little mining up in Nevada, silver mostly," Trace said.

"I wouldn't have pegged you for a miner."

Trace shrugged and didn't say anything.

"In fact, if I'd been asked to guess what you do, I would have said gun for hire."

Trace stopped chewing his steak and looked up at Mitch. "Now, what makes you say that?"

"The way you wear your gun, Trace. It's pretty obvious."

Trace chewed, swallowed, then grinned. "Shit, Mitch. I never could pull one over on you."

"Are you wanted for any killings?"

A dark shadow passed over Trace's face briefly; then his expression cleared. "No. I'm as innocent as a newborn."

Mitch doubted that but he couldn't argue until he heard back from the Tucson sheriff.

J. Paxton Reid came into the café, spotted Mitch and Trace, and came over.

"Sheriff, I hear you had a little problem at the Bad Dog earlier today."

"Alvin got shot."

Reid pulled a chair up and sat down. He caught Ellie's eye and nodded to the buffalo steaks. "What happened?"

"This man"—Mitch nodded to Trace and introduced him—"caught Alvin cheating at cards. Alvin started to go for his gun but Trace is faster. He only winged Alvin to discourage him."

Reid looked at Trace, assessing him. "Maybe he'd like to be your temporary deputy."

Mitch stopped eating and shook his head, glancing over at Trace, whose face remained impassive. "Oh, no, Mr. Reid, I think Trace will be moving on soon."

Ellie set down a plate of food in front of Reid and refilled coffee mugs all around. "You two know each other from before?"

Trace smiled. "Why, yes, Mr. Reid. We grew up together."

Reid grinned. "Ah, so you knew our sheriff when he was a little shaver."

Mitch didn't like the direction of the conversation. He stood up. "I'd better go check in at the telegraph office. I'm expecting a message from Tucson."

Reid sobered and gestured for Mitch to sit. "We won't talk about you anymore. But I want you to stay while I talk to Mr. Beaumont here." Mitch reluctantly sat back down and took another sip of coffee. Reid flagged Ellie down again. "Darlin', get these gentlemen some of that good pie of yours."

Mitch wasn't going to turn down another piece of peach pie. Jewel entered the café a few minutes later and came over to the table. "Hi, Mitch," she said; then her eyes strayed to Trace Beaumont.

Trace had stood up upon her approach and he stepped over to offer her a chair. "Miss Reid, you are joining us, I hope."

She smiled and sat. Mitch kept from rolling his eyes. He noticed Reid appraising the situation between his daughter and Trace Beaumont. "I see you two have already met."

Jewel turned to her father and smiled. "Yes. Earlier. Mitch introduced us."

Mitch watched the wheels turn in Reid's head. Reid smiled and turned back to Trace. "As I was saying earlier, Mr. Beaumont, our sheriff here could use a hand for a few days. His regular deputy has gotten his ankle twisted and has to stay off it for about a week. Would you be able to stay in town that long?"

Trace hesitated. "Well, I wasn't going to stay here for more than the one night."

Ellie brought thick slabs of peach pie and sat them down in front of Mitch and Trace. Jewel nodded to her. "Same, Miss Reid?" Ellie asked.

"Thanks," Jewel said. Ellie went off to get another plate.

"Mr. Reid," Mitch said, "I'm sure Mr. Beaumont has someplace to be. We can't go asking him to change his plans. This isn't his concern."

Reid looked thoughtful, then turned to Trace. "Is that true? Do you have plans that can't wait?" Reid asked.

Trace's expression became wary as he looked back and forth between Reid and Mitch. It was clear that he was sizing up the situation. "Well, I do have some plans, but I might be able to put them off."

Reid clapped him on the shoulder and said, "Hell, why don't you think on it tonight and give us your answer in the morning."

"All right, thank you, Mr. Reid. I'll do that."

Mitch shot a look to Trace. He didn't want Trace's help. When he had a feeling that he just couldn't shake, he knew enough to pay attention to it.

On the one hand, there was no talking Reid out of something once he got his mind set on it. On the other hand, maybe there would be an advantage to staying in close contact with a suspicious party like Trace Beaumont. Mitch knew there was something beyond Trace's admission that he was a gun for hire. He was trouble.

Chapter Four

After dinner, Mitch went over to the general store, but Abner had gone home. Mitch would have to wait until tomorrow to get any telegraph that might have come by for him.

He wandered the streets of Paxton, making sure the rowdy drunks stayed within the law and didn't shoot up any saloons.

When he'd walked the streets for a few hours, Mitch went back to his room and tried to get some sleep. It was the middle of the night when someone pounded on his door. "Sheriff! Sheriff! Wake up!"

Mitch stumbled out of bed and, because he recognized the voice as female, he slipped into a pair of pants.

It was one of Fanny Belle's girls. She had once been pretty but now she had a permanent weary look. Her name was Mary and she was wearing clothes that regular people wouldn't consider respectable—a threadbare robe and a cotton shift underneath it. If he stared real hard, Mitch could see about everything that Mary had to offer. But her expression told him she had urgent business.

Mitch ran a hand over his face to clear off some of the sleep. "What's the matter?"

"We got a customer's cut one of the girls. She's over at the doc's, but Fanny Belle's holdin' him off with a shotgun."

Mitch wouldn't want to be on the receiving end of Fanny Belle's shotgun. As he made his way down toward Fanny Belle's tent with Mary in tow, he half expected Trace Beaumont to be the man who cut the girl.

Instead, it was a wiry young guy with a mean expression. Fanny Belle glanced over at Mitch as he entered the tent. The customer was clearly drunk, and a mean drunk, at that.

"This him?" Mitch asked Fanny Belle.

The man had light brown hair, gray eyes, and large front teeth. But the thing about him that struck Mitch more than anything else was his slender wrists and large hands. Upon closer inspection, he saw the lines burned into the man's face from riding all day long in the sun. He realized that this man was not the sixteen-year-old that he had originally thought he was.

"I want this son of a bitch out of my tent. And he's not welcome back," she said.

"Did he pay the girl?"

Fanny Belle laughed, but there was no humor there. "He says she didn't give him his money's worth, so she don't deserve to be paid. And if she's not paid, I'm not paid."

"She's a goddamn whore," the man spat at Mitch

and Fanny Belle. Mary had slipped away, back to her bed.

"Of course she's a whore, you plug-ugly varmint," Fanny Belle said in clipped tones. "That's what you pay her for."

"Well, I couldn't get it up, so why should I pay her?" he asked.

"So that's her fault?" Fanny Belle asked spitefully, fingering the trigger of the shotgun. She aimed the shotgun at the man's privates. The man's eyes widened and Mitch stepped in, moving the shotgun barrel away from the customer.

"Get that whore away from me," the man demanded. "She's crazy!"

"Where did he cut your girl?" Mitch asked Fanny Belle, ignoring him.

"On the neck. He missed her face by an inch."

Mitch turned back to the man. "Where's your poke?"

"Don't have a poke. Ain't a miner."

Mitch realized he'd seen this man before, outside the Bad Dog. He was the man who walked past Trace Beaumont and seemed about to say something to him.

"You're new in town?"

"Just passing through," the man said, clearly unhappy he had to part with any information at all.

"Why don't we go over to the jail; you can clear your head with a night in a cell."

"It wasn't my fault she made me mad," the man said. Mitch relieved him of his gun and accompanied the man to the jail.

"It wasn't her fault you couldn't act on your intent," Mitch pointed out. But he knew he was talking to a drunk and any reason he used wouldn't stick.

When they got to the jail, he asked the man to empty his pockets. Fanny had handed over the man's gun, which she'd taken when he entered to do some sportin' with the woman of his choice.

"What's your name?"

"Sturms. Henry Sturms."

After escorting Henry to his home for the night, Mitch locked up Henry's gun and the knife he'd used on the prostitute in the lock box. He went through the man's coinage and paper money, duly recording it on paper. He put some of the money in his pocket and locked the rest away in a drawer of his desk, labeled with the man's name.

When he went back to Henry's cell, he showed the man the paper, pointing out the discrepancy in money.

"Hey! That's my money. You don't have no right to take any for yourself."

"You cut that girl," Mitch explained, "and she had to go to the doc to get sewn up. It's about a dollar a visit. Plus you owe her for her time and the time she'll probably take to heal." He showed Henry where to sign, and Henry reluctantly made an X to show he understood that the sheriff had his money and valuables locked up until he was released. Mitch folded up the paper. "I'd say you got off pretty cheap, so far. I'll have to ask the girl if she wants to press charges. If she does, then you'll have to wait for the circuit judge in this jail cell, which could take a couple of weeks at the least. Meantime, you get meals courtesy of the city of Paxton and you don't have to pay no rent."

Mitch turned the lock on the cell. Henry looked at his surroundings, the cot in the corner, the thundermug, and the desk and chair.

All the fire seemed to have gone out of him. The reality of his situation had sobered him up. He shrugged and sighed, then sat on the edge of the cot, resigned to his circumstances for the moment. "Guess it could be worse. But I'd hoped to be out of town by tomorrow. If you can see your way clear to telling the girl that, I'd 'preciate it. Might help her make up her mind in my favor."

Before Mitch left the cell area, he turned back to Henry. "By the way, you know a man named Trace Beaumont?"

Henry started. "What makes you think I know some man named Beaumont?"

Mitch smiled. "I passed you on your way into the Bad Dog this afternoon and Beaumont was with me. You looked like you knew him, but he walked by you as if you were a stranger."

Henry scowled. "What difference is it to you? It was probably your imagination."

"I've been told I don't have much of an imagination," Mitch said mildly. He turned the kerosene light out before locking the door to the cell area. "Night."

The next morning, Mitch checked on his prisoner. He also brought a plate of eggs and bacon and a mug of coffee from Ellie's Eat Here. Henry Sturms's bloodshot eyes and day-old whiskers didn't help his already rumpled appearance. Mitch wanted to keep him until he talked to the girl. He explained his situation to the prisoner.

"If she don't press charges, you gonna run me out of town?" Henry asked.

"Are you used to bein' run out of town?"

Henry squinted in thought for a moment. "Just as-kin'."

"You were heading south?"

"Yup." Henry was real talkative.

"Where'd you come from?"

He looked suspicious. "Why you askin' all these questions?"

"Why're you avoidin' all these questions?" Mitch asked.

"Boulder."

Mitch raised his eyebrows.

"Colorado. You asked where I come from."

Mitch rolled a smoke and thought on it for a while. He wondered about Henry Sturms.

He didn't get a good feeling about him either. And the way he was looking at Trace Beaumont when they passed outside the Bad Dog yesterday left Mitch with a bad taste that even his cigarettes couldn't cover up.

After he ate his own breakfast, Mitch brought a plate Ellie had fixed over to his deputy. Alky was sitting up in bed.

"Damn, I'm bored. Don't like sittin' around, doin' nothin'."

"You'll be up and out of here before you know it," Mitch said. Just because he felt sorry for his deputy, he related his day to Alky, including meeting up with his old friend Trace Beaumont.

Alky screwed up his face at the mention of Beaumont's name. "Seems to me I've heard that name in connection with a murder or two. It's a ways back, though. He was a gun for hire, all right. And he was excused for the killing."

"That would fit with my impression of him," Mitch

replied. "He wears his guns low. Just seems to be a gun for hire."

"Trust that feeling, Mitch," Alky said, shaking his head. "From hearin' you talk about him, I ain't gettin' a good feeling 'bout this man either, and I never met him."

"Well, Reid wants me to hire him as a temporary deputy to fill your shoes for a while."

Alky thought on that for a minute. Mitch rolled two smokes and gave Alky one. "Just watch your back," was his deputy's advice. "I never met Beaumont, but he could be one dangerous son of a bitch."

After he left Alky's room, Mitch went over to the general store. Abner worked at the general store when he wasn't operating the telegraph. A large, rawboned Swede with a shock of white-blond hair and bifocals, Abner looked up from his desk in the back of the store when Mitch approached.

"Got a reply from Tucson," he said, thumbing through a sheaf of papers. He singled a sheet out of the pile and handed it to Mitch.

"Thanks, Abner."

The message from Sheriff MacLean read that he couldn't find any information on Trace Beaumont at the moment, but he would let Mitch know if he came across anything.

Mitch thought on it and sent another telegram. This time, he sent it to Denver, Colorado.

He went over to Reid's mining office. Reid wasn't there, but Jewel was there with Bill Carson, the manager.

"He's gone to the mine, Mitch," Jewel said. "Can it wait?

"I'd better go talk to him now. It's pretty quiet in town right now anyway. All the drunks are sleeping off the effects of last night."

As he turned to leave, Jewel called out, "I'm making fried chicken and fresh rolls for the social. Pumpkin pie, too."

Mitch went over to Neely's to get his horse saddled. He rode over to the mine and found Reid in conversation with the new engineer, Shorty MacClellan. They were consulting a map of the mine.

"Shore up that wall, then. Get one of the fellows in town to help you," Reid was saying.

"All right, Mr. Reid," Shorty replied, rolling up the map and tucking it in a side saddlebag of a nearby horse.

"Sheriff," Reid greeted Mitch. "You've come a long way to talk to me. Can't be good news."

"It's not. That Beaumont fellow, he's a gunslinger. Alky recalls his name in connection with some murders."

"In this territory?"

Mitch paused, then shook his head. "He's not sure where, but it wasn't here. I'm not sure I'd be comfortable with him as my deputy."

Reid thought a bit. "Well, if you think you can do the job by yourself till your deputy is back on his feet, that's fine. Saves the town some money."

Mitch nodded. "We'll see."

"Just keep in mind that you have my consent to hire on a temporary deputy if needed."

Mitch left Reid and Shorty and headed back to town.

Chapter Five

The stagecoach rolled in about midafternoon. It stopped in front of the fancy hotel, the Gold Dust. A number of people were milling around outside of the hotel, waiting for the stage to arrive. Some waited for passengers, others waited for packages or letters or money, some just waited out of boredom or curiosity. Only one person waited to make sure the stage arrived intact. Mitch dropped the end of his hand-rolled cigarette in the dirt and crushed it with his boot heel.

He watched from the corner of the hotel building as a young woman stepped out and shyly looked around. A man Mitch recognized as a miner who'd done pretty good with his claim lately, stepped forward and started to talk to her. Mitch recalled that one of the miners had talked about sending for a mail-order bride. This must be the woman. He watched as the miner found her bags, picked them up, and the pair walked down the street to the other, less-expensive hotel, the Blue Rooster.

Several people were there to pick up packages, Ellie West, Sam Neely, and Bill Carson included. Neely walked by Mitch.

Neely greeted him. "Hey, Sheriff. Finally got some new bits and reins. Let me know if you need a new bit for your horse."

Mitch nodded, crossing his arms, and felt the sun beat down on his back. He watched Bill Carson help Ellie West load two crates of canned goods onto her wagon. He roused himself to go help them. Then he helped Bill load his own wagon with a couple of small crates of his own.

The driver walked toward him. "Sheriff."

Mitch nodded. "Have any trouble on the road?"

"Nope." The driver was a fellow called Witts. "Got somethin' for you, though." He handed Mitch a packet of wanted sheets. "The sheriff in Tucson asked me to get these to you."

"Much obliged."

"Um, listen, Sheriff, there's somethin' the sheriff down in Tucson told me to warn you about." He waited a beat. "The Hayes gang escaped."

Mitch lifted an eyebrow. "How'd that happen?"

"A new deputy turned his back and left the cell door open. They was to be hanged as soon as the circuit hangman got around to Tucson. Been a lot of murders this year."

"Does anyone know which way they're headed?" Mitch asked, recalling the promise Pen Hayes had made to him as Mitch left the courtroom.

Witts shrugged. "The sheriff's afraid they might be headed this way."

"Pen Hayes was overheard to say that if they escaped, he was gonna kill you. Said it several times, I guess. An' they tore up that place pretty good when they broke out—put that new deputy in the surgery."

"Thanks, Witts." Mitch pushed off from the building.

"You want to see another part of the country?" Witts grinned. He waved to his stagecoach. "We're leavin' in a few hours."

"Thanks. I don't intend to leave."

Witts shrugged. "Your funeral." He turned to help a woman with her bags.

Mitch headed back to his office. He was troubled by the fact that the Hayes gang was out and looking for him, but he couldn't leave Paxton for a number of reasons. The first reason was that even if he left, the gang would come in and do some damage, maybe kill a few innocent people just for fun. They weren't totally right in the head, he was sure of that. The second reason he couldn't leave was that he didn't back down from something like this. It was his problem and he would take care of it, not leave it for someone else to clean up.

The last reason was a very good one, and almost moot, in his opinion, although it caused him no end of aggravation: J. Paxton Reid held a signed confession of murder on him. It wasn't a real confession—Mitch had written and signed it as a way to get paid for going after a man who had stolen money from Reid, but it looked as if it were a confession. It was the way Reid had gotten Mitch to settle down here in Paxton and become sheriff. He was well paid, well liked, and was even getting to the point where he felt accepted here. But he was still bound by what Reid held over him. If he left, Reid might turn in the confession to other law officers and Mitch would spend the rest of his life a hunted man.

Now the Hayes gang was coming to town. Mitch couldn't leave even if he wanted to. The gang would kill citizens at random—at least Mitch believed Pen was crazy enough to do so if he didn't find the sheriff in town. And he knew that Pen's brother Elmer wouldn't try to stop him. The whole gang, from what he had observed the day they were captured, didn't have a conscience among them. Even if Rolly had a conscience, he was too stupid to recognize it, and Pen and Elmer were just pure bad news.

Mitch rolled another cigarette and smoked it. He thought some. Then he walked over to the *Paxton Gazette* to talk to Harvey Radin. Radin was a smooth-faced man, not too tall, not too short. "Hey, Sheriff. What brings you here?" Radin had rolled into town at the same time Mitch had a year ago. Someone was killing miners and Mitch had just been forced into taking the job as sheriff. Reid had immediately taken Radin over to an empty building that had been built for a butcher shop. But Dick Porter, the butcher, had died before he was able to set up shop. So Radin started up his newspaper and helped Mitch get information out to the people of the town, information Mitch wanted the killer to know.

"The Hayes gang."

Radin nodded, took up a pipe from a stand on his copy desk, and lit it. "What do you want to know?"

"Tell me what you know about them."

Radin squinted when the smoke drifted toward his eyes. He puffed harder. "They've robbed banks in towns from Colorado to New Mexico. They were captured just outside of Tucson—" He stopped and smiled. "You were in on the capture, weren't you, Sheriff? That was big news and I covered it."

Mitch nodded. "They just escaped."

Radin raised his eyebrows.

"They're headed this way."

"On purpose?" Radin was quick on the uptake.

"Pen Hayes threatened to kill me as I was leaving the courtroom. I just got a warning from the sheriff in Tucson."

"Maybe you could leave town."

"If you recall, the Hayes gang likes to kill people. What do you think they'll do if they come here and find out I've left?"

Radin nodded. "I see your point. You need to get the citizens together."

Mitch shook his head. "It's not their problem."

"It will be when the gang comes to Paxton. Can you head them off?"

"I'd have to circle around, pick up the trail, and try to get to them before they get here."

"How long you think you have?"

Mitch shook his head. "I probably have a day or two. They're going to take their time, avoiding the better-used trails. MacLean's probably already out there looking for them."

Radin's eyes twinkled. "But you're not tracking for MacLean."

Mitch shrugged. "There are other good trackers.

Sheriff MacLean knows I need to protect Paxton right now." He thought of another subject, one that had ended up on the back burner of his mind after he heard about the escape. "You ever hear of a Trace Beaumont?"

Radin thought about it. "Sounds familiar. I'll have to think on it for a bit."

"How about a Henry Sturms?"

The newspaperman squinted in thought. He shook his head. "Can't say as I know him."

Radin promised to look Mitch up if he thought about where he heard Beaumont's name before. Mitch left and went back to his office.

When he got back to the jail, he took the new wanted posters and went through them, taking down old ones and putting updated posters in their place. The Tucson sheriff had sent a list of the latest outlaws caught, hanged, or shot dead. He came across the Hayes gang sheets, folded them, and put them aside.

Trace Beaumont walked in and sat down in a chair across from Mitch. He put his boots up on the desk.

"You busy, Sheriff?" Trace grinned.

"Working," Mitch answered shortly.

"Heard you had a visitor in your cells last night."

"Friday nights men tend to get a little drunk and sometimes they do stupid things." It reminded Mitch that he ought to visit Fanny Belle and the girl who got cut, give her the money and all. "What can I do for you?"

"No, it's not what you can do for me, but what I can do for you."

Mitch waited.

"I'm takin' your mayor up on the offer to be a temporary deputy."

Mitch folded his arms and sat on a corner of his desk. "I appreciate the offer, but I can handle this town just fine for a few days, Trace. You go on and head on out. I thought you had a particular destination in mind."

Trace shrugged. "A few days won't make a difference."

Mitch waited. He rolled a smoke, thought about it, and rolled a second one for Trace. They smoked in silence for a minute. Mitch got the impression that Trace didn't like long silences, so he stretched it out as far as he could.

Trace finally spoke. "The news is out, Mitch. You got troubles coming this way, don't you?"

Mitch raised his eyebrows. Big news traveled around Paxton just fine by word of mouth. It was a wonder Harvey Radin could make a living as a newspaperman around here. "What makes you think that?"

"Talk around the town is that the Hayes gang broke out of the Tucson jail and they're headed this way. Just to kill you."

The door opened just then and Jewel came in, breathless. "Mitch!"

Mitch nodded to her and stood. Trace got out of the chair and touched his new hat. "Miss Reid. It's good to see you again." He indicated that the chair was free.

Jewel glanced at him and nodded briefly, but ignored the chair. She turned back to Mitch. "I heard about that gang. They're comin' after you, aren't they?"

Mitch nodded. "Probably."

"Why didn't they go after Sheriff MacLean?"

"He has too many people around him. I'm in a small mining town, easier to get to."

"Not just that but Sheriff MacLean and his posse might not have found them if you hadn't found out they double-backed," Jewel pointed out. "How long till they get here?"

"A few days. They're going to try to shake the posse first. Maybe go up north before riding down here."

"That would make them too tired to lift a gun, let alone try to find you," Trace said with a grin. He walked over to Jewel. "I'm going to be helping Mitch as his deputy for the next few days. I hope I see more of you."

Jewel smiled. "Maybe you'll be here long enough for the social."

"I wouldn't miss it."

"I have to get home and make supper for my father." She said good-bye and left.

Trace held his arms out. "Go ahead and deputize me, Sheriff."

Mitch hesitated. "Before I do, I need some answers to a few questions."

Trace nodded, sobering slightly. "Go ahead."

"You didn't come here alone, did you?"

"No, I didn't."

"Henry Sturms rode into town with you?"

"We rode in together, along with another man named Mort Keegan." Trace crossed his arms and looked down. "Look, Mitch, I know we ain't good friends and all. And I know you don't approve of how I once made my living. Yeah, I was a gun for hire, and I had some troubles—the relations of the men I was hired to kill made trouble for me. But I always played fair. I never shot anyone in the back or ambushed 'em."

"What I'm worried about is that you're here to kill someone. If you are, I want you to know that I will do everything I can to stop you, and if that fails, I'll have to take you in to stand trial here. I don't want any more killings in my town."

Trace held up his hands. "I'm done with killing for money. The men I killed weren't no angels, but the trouble I got into convinced me to change my ways."

Mitch finished his smoke and crushed out his cigarette.

"Tell you what, Trace, you and Mort get deputized and help me find the Hayes gang. Then you can move on. I need help routing out the Hayes gang and bringing them back to Tucson." He looked up at Trace and held his gaze for a moment.

Trace nodded. "Deal." He crushed out his cigarette as well and stuck his hand out. Mitch took it and they shook.

Mitch took one of the deputy badges out of the drawer and swore Trace in.

"Go find Mort and we'll leave tomorrow."

"What about Henry? He still in a cell? He's good with a gun. You can't find better." It was meant to be reassuring, but Mitch filed the information away for later.

"I have to talk to the girl he cut. We'll see."

Once Trace was gone, Mitch went over to Fanny Belle's to deliver the money. Fanny pointed to the panel crib where the girl was staying. She'd been put in a corner of the tent and a line stretched across the tent. Sheets held on by clothespins hung down to create some privacy for the girl. Her name was Madge and she was a young dark-haired girl, maybe part Indian— he couldn't tell in the darkness of the tent, even in daylight. A dirty bandage covered her neck.

"Hello, Sheriff," Madge said. A tear leaked out of the corner of her eyes. "Thank you for putting that bastard away."

"Can't keep him long unless you press charges. What do you want to do?"

She sighed and picked at an invisible thread. "Don't know, Sheriff. It's my word against his. Depends on the circuit judge we get."

Mitch rolled a smoke. "Here's my problem, Madge." He told her about the Hayes gang, how they were heading this way.

She listened, then asked, "What's that got to do with this bastard?"

"My deputy's laid up, and I need to gather a posse quick to go after the Hayes gang before they get here. If they get to Paxton, chances are they'll shoot up the town and hurt an awful lot of people just to get to me. This fellow came in with a man I deputized a while ago and he assures me Henry's good with a gun."

Madge thought about it, then nodded. "He wouldn't have gotten much time for the likes of me anyway." Meaning she was just a whore and the judge would most likely think she deserved what she got. She looked at Mitch. "If he agrees to help you out, Sheriff, I'll drop the charges."

Mitch handed her the money he'd taken from Henry's belongings. "This oughta help you out a bit."

She took it and quickly counted it. "It oughta," she

agreed. She smiled at Mitch. "You been a real gentleman to me, Sheriff. If you ever want to go sportin', I'll be here. Won't charge you none, either."

"Thank you, Madge."

Chapter Six

Mitch left Fanny Belle's and went over to Ellie's Eat Here for a meal. Today she was serving buffalo stew. Ellie brought a mug of strong coffee with the meal of stew and freshly made bread and Mitch sat and ate and thought.

He thought about the Hayes gang. Mitch had sized up the Hayes gang at their trial, and it appeared to him that Elmer Hayes was the leader, and he was less crazy than his brother was. Elmer hadn't appeared to be stupid when Mitch met him, and being a smart man, he probably realized that making a beeline for the man he'd sworn to kill made no sense. It would be best to hide out in the mountains for a few days, maybe a week, until the posse got tired of looking for them and gave up. Then the gang could go about their business without looking over their shoulders. So Elmer had probably figured all this out before they escaped.

The best way to get to Paxton from Tucson was to

go straight north, skirting the mountains. There were no rivers to cross, so it would be hard to cover up any tracks made in the sand. That would be the way the posse would expect the gang to travel, but Mitch predicted that the Hayes gang would stay off the well-known trails and go through the mountains where they could lose the posse in a day or so. They might have to stop in a town to get supplies, or might even risk holing up in a town for a few nights. Mitch knew the area fairly well and figured Hayden was a likely town for the Hayes gang to ride into.

Mitch went over to Reid's office again for another talk. Jewel was adding columns of numbers, but she looked up and smiled. Her father was sitting at his desk, going over some papers.

"Must be serious," Reid said.

"It is. The Hayes gang escaped before the hangman got to Tucson, and they're headed this way."

Reid raised his eyebrows. "So I heard. You better get a posse together and try to meet them outside of town."

"I don't know how long I'll be gone," Mitch said. "I'd have to take Trace Beaumont and two of his friends with me."

"You can't get anyone else to help you?" Reid asked.

Mitch shrugged. "Is anyone else in town good with a gun?" He knew there were some miners who could handle a gun easily, but getting them away from their claims to hunt down criminals for much less money wouldn't be very likely. Besides being paid less for real work, hunting down outlaws was dangerous and could get a fellow killed a lot more easily than mining for gold.

Reid frowned. "I'll think on it."

"We have to head out pretty soon. They escaped this morning, and Witts just told me about an hour ago."

"They could be here by now."

Mitch shook his head. "They have to avoid the posse from Tucson, and they want to catch me with my guard down. They'll probably wait a couple of days, thinking I'm going to relax my defenses."

Reid sighed. "Mitch, get a posse together. Tell your boys if they get the Hayes gang, there should be some reward money cut loose for them from Tucson, and I'll add some to sweeten the reward a bit."

"I'll tell them." Mitch hesitated, wanting to tell Reid what he'd just discovered among the old wanted posters, but he decided to leave it for a while because he wasn't sure of what he'd discovered.

Jewel wasn't in the outer office when he left.

Mitch went back to the jailhouse. Trace was there and had let Henry Sturms out of his cell. Henry was checking his gun. In the corner of Mitch's office sat an older man with an unkempt salt-and-pepper beard.

Henry looked up and grinned. "Hope you don't mind, Sheriff. I'm checking my property."

"How did you get into the gun box?"

Henry took out a straight piece of wire that had a bend at the end. "I got a few talents." He grinned.

Mitch wasn't sure he wanted to know what Henry's other talents were. He told Henry that he'd talked to the whore and she had agreed to drop charges if he rode with Mitch to get the Hayes gang.

Henry nodded. "I'm ready to go. My horse is at the livery across the street."

"Neely's. So is mine. I have to get a few supplies for us, and I have to check on my deputy, then we'll go." Mitch turned to Trace and nodded toward the other man. "This is your third member?"

"This is Mort Keegan. And he can handle a gun, all right."

Mort was returning the favor, studying Mitch. He touched his hat. "This is your friend, Trace? Looks Injun to me."

"My father was Apache," Mitch said evenly.

Trace shot a look at Mort. "Don't mind him, Sheriff."

Mitch took Trace aside. "Seems bound for trouble, too. Maybe we should leave him here."

Trace shook his head. "We traveled together from Colorado."

"You're responsible for him," Mitch said. He looked over at Henry again, who was slumped in his chair, staring at the floor. He seemed bored. "You said he can handle a gun? Can he shoot the side of a barn?"

Trace nodded. "He's good. So's Mort. You couldn't do better with a posse than me and my friends, Sheriff."

Mitch took his makings out and rolled a smoke. "Glad to hear it. Mr. Reid said there would be reward money coming from Tucson for the capture of the Hayes gang, and he would add to it as well. We have to bring back proof."

He turned to Mort. "Tell you what—you ignore the fact my father was Apache and we'll get along fine."

Mort squinted at him as if he thought Mitch was making fun of him, but finally decided he was serious.

"I wasn't bothered by you being a half-breed, son, just askin' a question."

Mitch swore them in and handed out badges.

"Let's go after them," Trace said, slipping his badge onto his shirt pocket. Mort and Henry got up and the three men went to the livery to liberate the horses while Mitch went over to the Blue Rooster to see how Alky was doing.

Alky was up and walking with a crutch when Mitch got to his room.

"I got tired of staying in bed all the time," Alky said.

Mitch explained what was going on.

When he was finished, Alky frowned. "Guess I'd better get over to the office."

"It's been pretty quiet. You shouldn't have to do more than sit outside the office and see how things are going from there."

"But if you miss the gang before they get here, they'll be shootin' up the town and I'm the only one here who can hit the side of a barn."

Mitch clapped Alky on the shoulder. "You'll do fine. And I'll make sure I get to them before they try to get to me."

Mitch went back to the office and made a list of supplies:

Hardtack
Dried meat
Bullets

He went to the general store and purchased items from his list, making sure he had enough bullets for Trace, Mort, and Henry. He was uneasy about traveling with three virtual strangers, but uneasier about tracking three outlaws on his own, especially three men who were bound and determined to kill him.

Trace and his companions brought the outfitted horses to the office and Mitch quickly packed the items he had just bought. Before he left, he went once more into the office and leafed through his discarded wanted posters, stopping at one to study it. Mitch read over the paper the Tucson sheriff had sent along just to make sure he read it right, then studied the wanted poster once more. He folded the poster and tucked it in his shirt pocket.

When he stepped outside, his three newly appointed deputies were waiting impatiently for him. He got on his horse and they headed down the street out of town. Mitch heard a woman calling him.

"Wait, Mitch!"

Mitch looked around and saw Jewel riding toward him down Main Street. She wore men's trousers and boots and she had a rifle in the saddle holster.

"What are you doing?" he asked.

"Going with you," she said. "I overheard you talking to my father."

"Miss Jewel," Trace greeted her.

"You can't go with us," Mitch said. The flash in her blue eyes told him he'd picked the wrong way to say it. He glanced at the other men. Trace maintained a respectful look, but Henry and Mort had grins as wide as the Rio Grande.

"This your little sister, Sheriff?" Mort asked. Henry just smirked.

Mitch ignored Mort's comment and took the reins of Jewel's horse, leading her away from the other men.

"Your father would have my hide if you came with us," he told her. "Four men and one unmarried woman out on the trail wouldn't be proper."

Her jaw was set. "You need help and I don't trust those three, Mitch. They're strangers. Someone has to watch your back and they don't look like they're watching anyone's back but their own."

"Trace is an old friend," Mitch said. "He saved me from drowning once. He's not out to kill me."

She glanced over at the three men. "That old one plain scares me. Has he said anything to you at all?"

"He insulted me," Mitch replied.

A half smile came to her pretty face. "Come on, Mitch. You need me."

"There is no one I'd rather have watch my back then you or Alky," Mitch told her, "but someone has to be here in Paxton. The gang might bypass us and someone has to watch out for the citizens. Alky is walking again, but with a crutch."

She looked into his eyes for a long moment, then slowly nodded. "All right. I'll stay. But you better come on back. That box social is coming up and someone's gotta bid on my fried chicken."

She turned her horse around, then turned in the saddle and said to the other men, "You watch the sheriff's back, you hear? My father will not be happy if he has to go to the trouble of finding a new sheriff. And you don't want to make him mad."

Trace watched her with amusement, tipping his hat to her. "Yes, Miss Jewel. We'll all come back alive."

As they were leaving town, Trace turned to Mitch. "That's some lady you've got there."

"We're friendly, but we're not keeping company."

Trace turned around and looked thoughtfully at Jewel's retreating back. "Is that so? Then maybe I have a chance."

Mitch wondered why he'd had to set the record straight. He knew Jewel could take care of herself, but he didn't like the way Trace watched the mayor's daughter. Mitch had gotten the impression that Trace was a man who liked women, and now he'd set his sights on Jewel.

Chapter Seven

The four men headed out of town, Mitch thinking about Trace and his connection to the other two men. He thought back to the wanted poster in his shirt pocket and wondered how it was possible for Henry to be alive. If he was right, the man who called himself Henry Sturms might be an outlaw named Billy the Kid. Billy had been shot down by another lawman, Pat Garrett, in Fort Sumner, New Mexico, a few years earlier.

Since he couldn't be positive that Henry was this outlaw, Mitch decided to bide his time.

"Miss Jewel sure is a pistol," Trace said, breaking into Mitch's thoughts.

"She's always been that way," Mitch replied. "Stubborn."

"Awful pretty, though. Is she a good cook?"

"She's fair." Mitch downplayed Jewel's cooking skills. He didn't want Trace to get any ideas. "Makes a good pie, maybe better than Ellie West's pie."

Trace took out a cigar, offered it to Mitch. Mitch took out his own makings and rolled a cigarette. Mort rolled his own as well. Henry leaned over to Mitch. "Mind?"

Mitch handed the smoke to Henry, figuring it might get him talking some, and rolled another for himself.

"You got any ideas, Mitch?" Trace asked.

"Plenty."

"Trace tells me you was a scout for Crook," Mort said.

"That's true enough."

"Then you oughta be able to track them fellas real quick," Henry added.

"Which way you figure they're comin', Mitch?"

"Through the mountains."

"The mountains!" Henry threw his smoke on the ground. "Damn. How the hell you supposed to track 'em in the mountains?"

Trace shot a serious look at his young companion. "Mitch oughta have a better idea than the rest of us."

"I know this area fairly well," Mitch admitted.

No more was said for several hours as each man kept to his own thoughts. The heat of the afternoon rippled before them, making the distant plateaus and cactus ripple like mirages.

They stopped for a break at a small way station. The owner had left for his monthly run for supplies, but Mitch knew that it was a working way station for stagecoaches and travelers. There was a watering hole for them to fill their canteens and a trough with fresh water for the horses.

"We should settle down for the night," Mort suggested. He looked around, squinting at the low sun in the sky.

"We still have some distance to cover," Mitch said. "And I'm familiar enough with this area to know where to camp."

"Well, I'm hungry," Henry said forcefully. He looked about to shoot someone if he didn't get fed. "The way station owner should be here to feed us."

Mitch shrugged. "There isn't a stagecoach coming by here till tomorrow, and he probably went to town to get some supplies. If you're not traveling on a stagecoach in these parts, don't expect the owner to be here."

"No wife?" Trace asked.

Mitch shook his head. "Died of typhoid fever a few years ago. Never remarried." He looked at the sinking sun. "We'd better continue. I want to get to the foothills of the mountains by tomorrow morning. We can camp in a few hours."

Henry sulked the entire time. Mitch finally took out some jerky and tossed it to the boy. "Here. This will curb your hunger until we make camp."

They made camp when the moon was full and had climbed almost halfway up the night sky. Mitch chose a patch of sand that was sheltered by saguaro cactus. He had collected pieces of dry wood and brush along the way in order to make a small campfire, big enough to cook some coffee. Mitch took out some of the hardtack and jerky and passed some around to everyone.

Henry made a face. "Again? Can't we catch a rabbit or snake or something?"

Mitch looked at Henry. "You want to go walking around out there till you find a snake asleep and kill it without shooting it, I'll skin it and Mort here will cook it."

"Why can't I shoot it?"

"It'll make noise and if the Hayes gang is anywhere within five miles of us, they'll know we're nearby." He stretched out on his saddle and bedroll, taking his makings out to roll a smoke. He lit it with a stick from the fire.

"They gotta know that now," Henry protested.

"Yeah, but right now, they only know the Tucson posse is after them," Mort said.

Henry turned to Trace. "Why do we have to do everything Mitch says?" he asked with a defiant expression.

"Mitch has done this before," Trace replied evenly. "We haven't. I'm with Mitch on this one."

A lock of light brown hair fell over Henry's eyes. He pulled out his gun. Mitch reached for his rifle. Trace's hand hovered over his gun, which was in his gun belt on the ground next to him. Mort looked uneasy.

Henry noticed everyone's reaction. "What? I'm checking my gun to make sure it's in working order."

"I'd feel better if you broke the cylinder before checking it over," Mitch said.

"You don't trust me?" Henry asked with a mocking look.

No one answered. Mitch offered to take the first watch. The others settled down for the night.

As Mitch was lighting his last cigarette before his watch ended, Trace joined him. "I'll take over from here."

"That's fine," Mitch replied. He took a moment to

watch the sky. The air was cool, but there was no breeze tonight. He'd seen a small fire a distance away earlier in the evening, but hadn't mentioned it because he wasn't sure if it was the Hayes brothers, the posse, or just some drifter. He made a note of the location so they could head that way in the morning.

"You haven't asked me much about what I've been doing since we both left our hometown, Mitch."

"I figured you'd tell me in your own time. Now's as good a time as any, if you want to tell me."

Trace squinted. "I got married. Sarah Jane. You remember her?"

Sarah Jane Hathaway had been a blond beauty whose parents owned the general store in town. All the boys, including Mitch, had been a little in love with her. Mitch, being half Indian, figured he'd never have a chance with her. But it made sense that Trace, a tall, handsome, able-bodied boy, would end up with Sarah Jane.

"Did you have any kids?"

Trace grimaced. "Yes and no. She took up with a lieutenant at the nearby fort. She was with child, but it was his. When the lieutenant got orders to transfer to another fort, she thought he'd want her to come along. But he didn't." Trace looked away briefly. "After the baby was born, she killed herself."

"Where's the baby?"

"With her parents. It was a little girl. They're raising her."

"You didn't stay around?"

Trace picked up a rock and threw it hard out into the desert. "I went after the lieutenant." He looked

Mitch straight in the eye. "I admit it, I killed him. But I gave him a chance to draw."

"You couldn't go back home?"

"No. Not after what I'd done. That little girl's mother was as dead as if the lieutenant had killed her with his bare hands. And my wife was dead."

"It didn't bother you that she took up with him in the first place?" Mitch wasn't sure how he'd react it he ever had a wife who was unfaithful to him.

"Hell. Of course I was angry. But I probably helped Sarah Jane along in her decision to take her life. If I hadn't been such a damned stubborn bastard, if I'd forgiven her, she might have been able to live with herself." He was silent for a moment. "But it ain't that I'm feelin' guilty about making Sarah Jane feel like she had to kill herself; I feel for that little girl who's gonna grow up without a ma or pa. And as she's growin' up, the other kids are probably plaguing her about not having a ma or pa."

"Why don't you go back there and get the kid, raise her yourself?"

Trace shrugged. "She's probably five or six by now. She's used to Sarah Jane's folks."

"Then it's been a while." Trace had talked as if only happened a few months ago, Mitch thought.

"I don't like to talk about it more than I have to. You wanted to know what I'd been up to." Trace grinned.

"After you killed the lieutenant, what did you end up doing?"

"Worked as a cattle detective for a time. Hired out to men who paid me to keep the peace with their neighbors." Mitch was aware that most cattle detectives weren't as upstanding as Trace made them out to be—most likely he killed a few men as a warning for others to stay out of his employer's way.

"How did you hook up with those two?" Mitch indicated Mort and Henry's sleeping forms with a nod.

Trace was evasive. "We were all heading in the same direction."

"That it? You said you hooked up with Mort in Colorado. What about Henry?"

Trace shrugged as he scanned the dark horizon. "Later."

"The kid is a little hotheaded."

Trace looked at Mitch, his expression unreadable in the darkness. "What makes you say that?"

"What he did to that girl back in Paxton."

"You mean that whore? She probably deserved it."

"I got both stories and actually she didn't deserve it." Mitch paused, looking out into the night. Then he said, "He reminds me a little of Billy the Kid."

He heard Trace stiffen slightly.

"That outlaw's dead, isn't he?" Trace asked. His voice was casual, but underneath, there was a tightness Mitch hadn't heard before.

"That's what the paper says. Can be wrong at times. Doesn't make no difference to me. I just get the feelin' there's more to Henry than meets the eye."

"And you don't think that of Mort?"

Mitch squinted in thought. "No. He didn't cut up a girl."

"Henry was drunk. He gets mean when he drinks."

"I don't want him drinkin' then when we get to the next town. I don't want trouble."

He saw Trace's shoulders relax a bit. There was a

hint of a smile on his face. "I guarantee Henry will be fine. He don't drink much. But we'd just come off the trail and I guess some of us gotta let off a little steam."

"If Henry's not Billy the Kid, he does have the law after him. Am I right?"

Trace took a cigar out and lit it, cupping his hand over the flame to keep from giving away their position. Mitch was bothered by the fact that Trace was so comfortable working this way. It was clear he had been on both sides of the law. But which side was he on now?

"We've all made mistakes. I've been making a living with my gun for so long now, it's hard to imagine making a living any other way."

"I never thought that I lived by the gun," Mitch said. "I always use it as a last resort. But it's true enough lots of folks out here live by the gun. I get the feeling there's more to Henry than there appears to be."

A wry smile. "Back to Henry again. You can't leave it alone, can you?" Again, a wary look from Trace.

"He may have been drunk when he cut that whore, and he seems to be a pleasant enough fellow...." Mitch shrugged and finished his smoke. "I once saw a pot of boiling water blow up. The lid had been screwed down tight and the heat turned up so high that the pressure inside just exploded. That's the feeling I get with Henry. He's going to explode someday, if he hasn't already. And I don't want to be around when he does. I get the feeling he'd prefer to shoot a man in the back than give him a chance to defend himself."

Trace's expression turned to stone. "You seem to have him all figured out, don't you, Mitch? Has he given you any reason to think that way?"

"Not really. I just noticed what Henry said and did

and I don't feel real comfortable going to sleep next to dynamite that's about ready to blow."

"What about Mort, what're your thoughts on him?" Trace sounded a little sarcastic now.

Mitch ignored the sarcasm. "I haven't had occasion to watch him. Just met him."

"And me?"

"I think you're here for a reason, but I haven't figured it out yet."

"You think I'm gonna shoot you in the back?"

Mitch thought about it. "Not yet. You still need me." He got up and stretched. "I'm going to turn in, I think. Wake me if there's a problem."

Mitch could feel Trace's eyes on his back as he headed back to the camp to get some rest.

Chapter Eight

Mitch and his posse were up early. They boiled what was left of the coffee from the night before and had another meal of jerky and hardtack. Henry was sullen, which was turning out to be not unusual in the morning, and the other men were silent. Trace didn't talk to Mitch any more than he had to.

They reached the foothills of the mountains by mid-morning. Henry and Trace began to head toward them, but Mitch stopped them.

"We have to go around the foothills like we're going to Tucson and pick up the trail from there."

The men rode for a time until Mitch stopped them again.

"Why don't you rest the horses while I go on ahead and pick up the trail. There's a watering hole over yonder." He pointed east. "You should reach it within thirty minutes."

Trace nodded. "We'll meet you there."

"How long do you think you'll be?" Mort asked.

"You should be able to make coffee and catch yourself something to eat before I get back," Mitch said. "If you run into Sheriff MacLean and his posse, let them know you're deputies working for me. The sheriff might wait with you, but then, he might decide they've searched enough for the Hayes brothers."

They parted ways and Mitch rode on, looking for signs of travel into the mountains.

It was an hour later when he found the sand recently disturbed. From the signs, it was more than one horse, and that was good enough for him. The Hayes gang had misdirected the sheriff's posse once before, and Mitch had little doubt that they had done so once again.

He headed back to the watering hole where he'd agreed to meet Trace and his men. They had cooked up some coffee and were roasting a rabbit.

Trace looked up. "You find 'em?"

"They went into the mountains about twelve miles southeast of here. Did the posse come by here?" Mitch dismounted and took his almost empty canteen over to the watering hole. He filled it up again.

Trace followed him. "No. Never saw them. You want to stay here and eat before heading out?"

Mitch shook his head. "I'd like to go now. You can follow me when you're done. It'll be at least a few hours before we catch up to them, by my reckoning." He headed back the way he came.

Shortly after he left, Mort joined him.

"That hardtack sure fills you up," he said. When he grinned, Mitch noticed he was missing a tooth near the front.

"Sure does."

"Trace and Henry will be along shortly. Henry wants to eat that rabbit and Trace wants to stay behind to make sure Henry puts out the fire right."

They fell silent. Mitch was troubled by the fact that other tracks crossed their tracks to the watering hole, and he suspected the posse had crossed paths with Trace, Henry, and Mort. Maybe they didn't meet, but Mitch got the impression that Trace was lying when he told Mitch they hadn't come across the posse. So why would Trace lie to him? The more men in the posse to go after the outlaws, the better the chances were of taking the Hayes outlaws alive. Of course, if Trace was worried about sharing any reward money, he might stretch the truth a bit.

Mitch put it in a corner of his mind and concentrated on tracking. Trace and Henry hadn't caught up to them, but he figured they would by the time he reached the foothills.

"Sure is thirsty work," Mort said. "Too bad there isn't a town around here. I sure could use a saloon about now."

"You should have filled up your canteen before we left the hole back there."

Mort squinted at Mitch. "You a teetotaler?"

"No, I like my whiskey," Mitch allowed. "But out here, liquor makes me thirsty and water doesn't." As a scout, he had learned this fact very quickly. Tom or Al might carry a small flask of whiskey for emergencies, but they didn't do much drinking when they were working. Some of the Apache scouts had problems with drink and they would bring bottles with them, but if they were unreliable, Crook cut them loose. The general liked his drink as much as the next man did, but he was all no-nonsense when it came to tracking Geronimo and his people.

The Apache wars were rumored to be over, but Mitch and his posse still skirted the area—and the Hayes gang was riding right into it, as far as Mitch could tell. He didn't like the idea of heading back into the area, but it was the fringe and they might be overlooked.

As with all government agencies, a lot of bragging went on about how the Arizona and New Mexico Territories had been cleared of Indians. The Indians had been sent to Florida, thousands of miles to the east, and from what Mitch had heard from other sources, Geronimo and his people were dying of disease and neglect in Florida.

Still, Mitch knew that a few Apaches had escaped the roundup of the last few years. When Crook had Tom Sieber give the bad news to the Apache scouts that they were about to be cut loose, most of the scouts wanted to be with their tribes and went quietly and cooperatively to Florida along with rest of the Indians. But some of the scouts had slipped away, not wanting to be shipped off to some faraway place. They'd rather take their chances in the desert than in a foreign place like Florida.

"How long have you been riding with Trace?" Mitch asked Mort.

"What did he tell you?" Mort sounded wary. It was clear that he was uncomfortable with lying, and he had probably been told to be careful about what he told Mitch.

"Everything."

Mort looked like he didn't believe him, and Mitch

grinned in response. Mort grinned back, but he was clearly uncomfortable with talking about Trace. Mitch switched subjects.

"How long have you known Henry?"

"Him," Mort grumbled. "That one is trouble." He was opening up.

"You must not know him very well."

"We picked him up about a week before we got to your town."

"Was Trace intending to go through Paxton?"

Mort looked wary again. "He knew it was on the way to Tucson."

"And Tucson was your final destination?"

Mort shrugged. "Actually, Trace suggested we bypass Tucson a few days before we got there."

"It sounds like you've been riding with Trace for a time."

Mort looked away. "Longer than Henry."

"Was Henry in trouble before Paxton? Did he cut any other whores or start any fights while he was drunk?"

Mort shrugged. "We only knew him a week."

This was already different from what Trace had told Mitch about knowing the two men. Apparently they hadn't gotten their stories straight, or Mort just didn't feel like lying. Trace acted as if he'd known Henry longer, and didn't answer Mitch when he was confronted with the possibility of Henry being a notorious dead outlaw named Billy the Kid.

"What makes you certain Henry is trouble?" And that was another thing Mitch found odd—Trace had appeared to distance himself from Henry when they passed right outside the Bad Dog, but now he acted as if it was all a mistake.

Mort frowned and scratched his whiskers. "I figure ol' Henry's gonna blow one of these days an' I don't want to be around when it happens. Someone's gonna get hurt." Mort glanced sideways at Mitch. "That whore found out, all right. Mean drunk, Henry is. I'm surprised that he cut an Indian whore. He likes Indians and Mexicans. Gets along real well with 'em. Speaks Mexican like he was one of 'em."

"That's reassuring," Mitch replied dryly.

"Don't get me wrong," Mort added hastily. "I ain't like that. A man is a man, white, black, or Mexican. I either like him or I don't. I don't like Henry, for example."

It was a point in Mort's favor, Mitch thought, but he didn't voice what he was thinking.

They came to the foothills and rested while they waited for Trace and Henry to catch up.

About thirty minutes later, the two other men and their horses appeared on the horizon.

"We gonna camp here tonight before moving on?" Henry asked.

Mitch shook his head. "I want to catch up to 'em. They may be camping somewhere in these hills early tonight. If not, they may ride till they get to Hayden, which is on the other side of the mountains." The area where the outlaws went into the mountains wasn't a long ride straight through, but it was a lot of up and down. Mules would work better than horses in the mountains, but the posse wouldn't be able to track down the Hayes gang as quickly.

As they entered the mountains, Mitch thought back

to when he tracked the Hayes brothers down before. He recalled the trial day and having coffee with Sheriff MacLean and the mention of the missing money. He wondered how many people knew that. Assuming the Hayes gang was captured with the missing money on them, would Trace and his men turn on Mitch for the money? He had no way of knowing until it happened. Mitch would just have to be watchful.

The night had become chilly, but it was still clear with enough light from the still-full moon and unclouded night sky to keep on riding. Henry complained briefly of the cold, but the other men hunkered down and stayed silent.

Following the outlaws' trail wasn't difficult—they should have posted signs telling the posse where they were going—it would have been less conspicuous. The posse came to rest again when Mitch knew they were reaching the foothills on the other side of the mountains. Before them stretched the desert, saguaro cactus rising up like sentinels in the darkness. The Table Mountains rose up against the brilliant night sky just beyond the foothills, providing a backdrop for the tiny boomtown, Hayden. Mitch had never been to Hayden, but he had heard about it from Reid. It was a copper and silver mining town that had beginnings similar to Paxton's.

"We'll camp here," Mitch said. The mountains sheltered their campfire from visibility. It would be a quick descent in the morning to the desert floor and the town beyond the Table Mountains.

Henry had brought along the rabbit. Mitch turned down a portion that Trace offered, not particularly enjoying the gamy taste. He stuck to the jerky and hardtack. They boiled the last of their coffee, then turned in. Mort took the first watch.

Mitch woke sometime later. He heard voices and looked around. Mort was asleep. Henry's and Trace's bedrolls were empty. Mitch assumed that this meant that one man was relieving the other of his watch.

"Are you sure it's with them?" Mitch recognized Henry's voice.

"It has to be. They wouldn't leave it behind even if there was a posse on their tail." The voices were soft, so Mitch couldn't be sure he was getting the entire exchange.

"What do we do about him?"

Mitch wasn't sure if Henry meant Mort or him or someone else.

"We'll deal with that when we come to it."

"We shouldn't have hooked up with that sheriff," Henry said. "He makes me nervous. We should get rid of him right now."

"We can't. We need him. He's a good tracker. It would take us longer to track them down without his help. Besides, the odds are better if there's more of us than them."

Mitch pulled his gun closer for reassurance. He thought about confronting them right now, handcuffing them and taking them to the Hayden jail, or maybe not doing anything until tomorrow morning when they rode into Hayden. It sounded to him as if they still felt they needed him, but with Henry expressing doubts about Mitch to Trace, Mitch wasn't sure how long Trace would consider him necessary.

There was little sleep for Mitch that night.

The next morning, they got up early, had the boiled

coffee left from the night before, and began the descent. Within an hour, they were back in the desert. The Table Mountains loomed over them as they entered the town of Hayden. It was early and Henry glanced at the rest of the men.

"I'm getting some grub. Something besides hardtack and jerky." He headed over to the first tent café.

Trace looked at Mort and Mitch. "What do you want to do?"

Mitch nodded to the two men. "Why don't you join Henry and I'll scout out the town. I'll meet you back there."

Hayden was similar to Paxton of a few years earlier. Lots of business tents with a few wooden and stone buildings dotting the town. One of the buildings was the sheriff's office. No one was there this early except the prisoners. Mitch tethered his horse to the hitching post outside and walked the main street. He spied a livery stable and went inside. The owner was there, watering the horses and making sure they had feed. He was a short, burly man with big ears and blond hair.

Mitch told him who he was. "Do you have a sheriff here in town?"

The man, whose name was Felix, shook his head. "We're looking. You want the job?"

Mitch smiled. "Couldn't leave Paxton. Who locks up the drunks?"

Felix laughed. "They lock themselves up. There's a couple of 'em who consider it home after they get good and drunk on a Saturday night."

"What about the angry drunks who shoot up the town?"

"We've all gotten pretty good with a gun," he replied. "The citizens usually take care of the trouble-makers."

"Did any travelers come into town yesterday? Three men." He described Pen and Elmer Hayes and Rolly Rollins.

Felix nodded. "Yeah, their horses are boarding here." He grinned. "Only boarding stable in town."

"Do you know where they're staying?"

"Sure. At the Silver Moon Hotel." He nodded toward the only built-up hotel on Main Street.

"Thanks."

Mitch walked down the street to the hotel and described the Hayes brothers to the clerk on duty, a young man who probably had not taken a straight razor to his cheeks yet.

"Yes, they're staying here." He looked down at Mitch's gun belt. "There's not going to be any trouble, is there? If there is, they just left to get something to eat."

Mitch figured the clerk wasn't giving him this information out of the goodness of his heart but because, if there was going to be any trouble, it wouldn't be at the hotel, where bullet holes would mar the walls and furnishings of the new building. He thanked the clerk anyway and headed back to the café. He noted the tents where EAT HERE signs hung. There were three on Main Street, including the one on the edge of town where Henry, Trace, and Mort were sitting right now.

Mitch rolled a cigarette and smoked it, thinking about what he'd heard last night and what he knew of the Hayes gang. He turned the information he'd gathered over in his mind, including the rumor that there used to be at least one other Hayes gang member. He wondered if it was Henry. Or it could have been Trace.

What Mitch had overheard last night was disturbing. He didn't think he could trust any of them, but of the three men he'd deputized two days ago, the one he knew the least, Mort Keegan, was the one he trusted the most.

He crushed his cigarette on the ground and walked back to the café. The tent had long tables with men sitting at them elbow to elbow. A woman was cooking at one end and her daughter was pouring coffee. Henry was working on a second plate of eggs and ham. Mitch could tell that because it was piled on top of his first plate.

The cook caught Mitch's eye and he nodded as he sat down.

"What did you find out?" Trace asked. He was finished with breakfast and was drinking more coffee and smoking a cigar. Mort was finishing his meal.

"They're here." He'd thought about it before he came back here. He couldn't keep the information to himself. At this point, they wouldn't need him if he told them that the Hayes gang was here. But if he did withhold information, they would eventually figure it out. And he needed them to help capture the gang.

Once the gang was captured, Mitch was thinking of locking up Trace and Henry as well, but he couldn't figure out what to charge them with. Talking about getting the money and not needing Mitch anymore wasn't good enough. They needed to act on what they talked about last night for him to arrest them.

"At the hotel?"

Mitch shook his head. A plate of fried eggs and ham and thick crusty bread was placed in front of him, along with a fork and knife. He got busy as the cook's daughter poured coffee and set the mug in front of him. "They're at one of the cafés right now doing the same thing we're doing."

Henry stopped eating, put his fork down, and started to stand up. "What are we waiting for?" he asked. "Let's go get 'em."

"I'd rather follow them out of town so citizens don't catch any bullets." Mitch dug into his breakfast. He was as tired as the others of hardtack and jerky, but he hadn't been complaining about it as loudly. He'd spent plenty of time sleeping under the stars when he was tracking Geronimo, and when he wasn't near the Army camp to get Cook's grub, he made do with whatever he'd been able to stuff in his saddlebags that didn't rot in the hot weather.

Henry sat back down but soon became fidgety. "We can get 'em here without anyone gettin' hurt, Sheriff. Let's go do your job."

Mitch stopped eating and looked up calmly at Henry, then over to Trace. "Seems to me you're suddenly eager to get 'em when your belly is full. They're not going far. I already told you I'd rather capture them outside of Hayden." He turned back to his meal. He could feel the heat of Henry's agitation on the back of his neck. Mitch kept eating with one hand, his other hand by his side.

Henry suddenly got up and paced back and forth like a caged mountain cat. Trace stepped in. "Let's go outside, Henry. This isn't the time or place to call attention to us. We're just the deputies."

Mort sat with Mitch, sipping the last of his coffee. He didn't say anything.

Trace came back and sat down. "Henry's stayin' out there till you're done."

Mitch stopped eating. "Trace, is there somethin' you haven't told me? I get the feelin' you didn't take this deputy job for no better reason than you had time on your hands." He glanced at the tent opening. "And that fella out there—when the time comes, will he do as I say or is he just gonna go off like a filed-down hair trigger on a six-shooter?"

Trace's mouth tightened. "He'll do as I say. We're here to pick up a little extra money, Mitch, and that's the God's honest truth."

Mitch wondered whose money Trace was planning to pick up—the posse money or the Hayes' gang money. Trace was good at hiding whatever his real purpose was for going along with Mitch, but Henry wasn't as good about hiding his true reasons.

One thing was sure—Mitch wasn't turning his back on Henry any time soon.

Chapter Nine

When Mitch stepped out of the tent café, Henry was gone. It was easy to figure out where he'd gone. He had stopped at the second tent café on Main Street heading back to the hotel, but it was at the third tent café that Mitch and the others found him. This café had a hand-lettered sign by the tent flap that announced FOOD.

The three men were too late to stop Henry from ripping open the tent flap and drawing his gun. A moment later, Mitch heard a few curses and growls from the customers in the tent; then it became quiet. Henry stepped back out, a scowl on his face. He holstered his gun.

"They weren't there."

"Must have gone back to the hotel," Trace said. "Let's go."

Mitch held up a hand. "I don't want a shootup at the

hotel. We'll wait and follow them out of town like I said before."

"But if we get them here, we can lock them up," Mort argued.

"If we face them here, there'll be a gunfight and innocent people could get in the way," Mitch pointed out.

"No more talk. You said your friend would be with us, Trace. I'm goin' in. Anyone with me?" Henry turned and strode toward the hotel.

Trace turned to Mitch. "He's not leaving us much choice, is he?" He followed Henry. Mort looked back and forth between Trace and Henry and Mitch, then followed Trace.

Mitch followed. He couldn't control a man who wanted a fight, and Henry was anxious for one. He just hoped the young man was as good with a gun as Trace had advertised. Otherwise he would be less one temporary deputy as well as any innocent bystanders who might get killed or injured if they got in the way. But at least he could follow the others and try to prevent bystanders from getting hurt.

When Mitch got into the lobby, the clerk at the desk looked worried. "Where did the other men go?" Mitch asked.

"Down the hall," the clerk said, pointing toward the door that led to a hallway. "But, really, we don't want any trouble."

"Then make sure no one comes into the hotel until we leave," Mitch instructed, showing his badge. "And if there's any shooting, keep your head down. Don't try to be a hero."

The clerk was wide-eyed by the time Mitch finished his instructions and could do little more than nod.

There was already a commotion going on by the time Mitch got to the end of the hall. The Hayes gang had had the presence of mind to request a room on the first floor for a fast getaway.

Raised voices exchanged heated words and Mitch only caught a few of them. "Where is it?" and "I'll see you in hell" were the last phrases he caught.

When Mitch got to the room, Henry was halfway out a window, his gun drawn, shooting at someone or something. Shots were returned and the bullets splintered the wooden window frame. This didn't seem to faze Henry, who leaned even farther out the window to return fire, Trace crowding him, almost pushing him out the window as the sound of hooves beat a fast retreat.

Mort was yelling something unintelligible, gun drawn, but unable to fire because the only space to aim was filled with Henry and Trace.

Mitch got their attention by yelling their names. "Trace! Henry! Mort!"

Mort had already holstered his gun. Henry muttered "Goddamn it!" and retreated into the room, and Trace silently withdrew from the window and expertly broke his bullet chamber to check his gun now that they were finished.

"What the hell were you doing?" Mitch asked.

"We were tryin' to catch the gang for you," Mort said.

Mitch let out a short, humorless laugh. "Damn, I would have done better goin' after them by myself. Consider yourselves cut loose. If you want to ride through Paxton on your way back from Tucson, I'll make sure you get paid for your time." He turned to leave the room.

"Mitch! Sheriff!" Trace came after him. Mitch paused but then kept walking away. Trace caught up with him. "What the hell is the matter with you?"

Mitch stopped and turned to face Trace. "The matter is that the only one of you that follows orders around here seems to be Mort and from the looks of that gunfight back there, I'll have three more dead bodies on my hands if I keep you and your friends around."

"What do you mean? We were just trying to get the Hayes brothers for you."

"Bustin' into a hotel room with blazin' guns *against* my orders, shootin' into the street at retreating outlaws—it was almost as if you were *tryin'* to let them get away." Mitch narrowed his eyes at Trace. "I told you I thought Henry was trouble and he proved me right back there. And Mort stood there like a big target—it's a miracle that none of you got shot with all the lead flyin'. And you, hell, I don't know what to think. You act like a gun for hire until you go after a man. If you really are a gun for hire, how do you stay alive—sneakin' up on your target and shootin' 'em in the back?"

Trace's expression became angry. "Watch what you're sayin', Mitch. We may have growed up together, but I never considered you a friend."

There was a silence between them. Mitch finally nodded. "I never thought of you as a friend either. I owed you my life, but I think this feebleminded action just finished my obligation."

"You've been actin' like you're suspicious of me all

the time, Sheriff, makin' comments about not trusting me or the others, especially Henry. Why don't you just come out and say what you're thinkin'?"

Mitch nodded. "All right. You're not being honest with me. The story I get from you is that you knew Henry before you knew Mort. But Mort tells me he rode with you from Colorado and you two picked up Henry along the way. Last night, I heard you and Henry talkin', and I think you know what I heard you sayin'. And when I walked up to the room a few minutes ago, you were having words with one of the Hayes brothers. Familiar words, like you knew them and they knew you. Maybe you're that fifth member of the Hayes gang, the one there's a rumor about. Maybe you didn't die when you rode with them, just disappeared. Maybe you were almost killed, but you survived and have been tracking them down to get your fair share." Silence fell as thick and bitter as molasses.

Trace's voice came out thick with anger. "You're wrong, and you can't prove a damn thing."

"I'm done with you." Mitch turned and walked out of the hotel room.

"Sheriff!" Trace called after Mitch.

Mitch stopped and turned around, fully expecting Trace to have pulled a gun on him. Instead, Trace strode down the hall toward him and stopped in front of him.

"You can't go after those men by yourself."

"I can and I will. I'd be safer by myself."

"You'll just end up being killed."

"I don't plan on that. I've faced worse odds and come out alive."

"Let me go with you."

Mitch studied Trace. He looked serious, but Mitch couldn't trust Trace. Still, if he didn't leave soon, he wouldn't be able to track down and capture the Hayes gang before the sun went down.

He'd been in worse situations by himself and come out alive. He knew there was a chance he might be hurt or killed, but that was part of his job. He thought about it and offered a solution to Trace.

"I wouldn't be a very smart lawman if I went up against the Hayes gang with a fellow like Henry behind me," Mitch replied. "He may be handy with a gun, but he'd be more likely to get me killed than if I go after them by myself. But thanks for the offer of help."

He started to turn away but Trace caught his arm. "You can't do this by yourself, Mitch. I know you have your doubts about me and Mort and your suspicions about Henry. I'll tell him to stay behind. I'll tell him they may double-back and I want him to stay here to make sure that doesn't happen." Trace's tone was serious.

Mitch stepped away from Trace. "I have to go now. If you want to come after me with just Mort, I'll welcome evening the odds. But I don't want Henry with you."

Trace looked as if he had more to say, but Mitch cut him off. "Follow me if you want to, but don't bring Henry." He could see Henry and Mort coming out of the hotel room now. He turned away and headed out of the hotel.

A few minutes later, he had determined the direction the gang had headed. By midday, he had picked up their trail. They were heading in a big circle, trying to lay a false trail that looked as if they were headed north when in fact they were slowly moving back south, possibly to Mexico or at least near the border.

Mort and Trace caught up with him as the sun was starting to descend in the west.

"I left Henry back in Hayden."

"He wasn't happy about it," Mort said, clearly enjoying himself.

"He's not going to follow us, is he?" Mitch asked.

Trace gave Mitch a long, even look. "No. He'll do as I say."

Mort chuckled to himself.

"We'll pick him up on the way back," Mitch replied. He told Trace and Mort what he suspected the Hayes brothers of doing. "We have to stop them by cutting west."

It meant going through Apache territory. Geronimo's surrender didn't mean that a few wild Apaches hadn't escaped the fate of most of their nation. In fact, the Apache scouts who had worked for General Crook several years ago had been fated to be shipped off to Florida with their tribe.

When Al Sieber broke the news to them, a few of the Apaches had disappeared that night. Since then, there had been a few sightings of small bands of renegade Apaches and it was believed that they lived off the land and stayed away from white towns. The Army still looked for them, but not as diligently now that Geronimo was no longer in the territory to lead them in raids and killings.

Mitch would rather run into renegade Apaches than Army men any day. He at least had a chance of talking to the Indians. Soldiers, as he well knew, would rather shoot first; then, if he was still alive, they'd ask him what business he had in the area.

"Say, this area looks familiar," Mort said, light dawning on his face. "I think I was here a few years ago. Ain't we headin' into hostile territory? I heard a few men have been killed out here."

"We are, but that was a few years ago. Any Apaches we meet will be as uneasy about us as we are of them."

Mort slowed his horse down. "Now wait just a damn minute."

Mitch turned his horse around to face Mort. Trace stayed back. "If you have a problem with where we're going," Mitch said quietly, "you can wait for us back in Hayden along with your friend." Mitch looked from Trace to Mort. "I'm not looking to get anyone killed here, but I gotta make up for lost time."

Trace nodded. "I'm with you."

Mort seemed to think about it, peering hard at Mitch, then Trace. He finally gave a short nod. "Guess it's better than goin' back to that town to wait with that young fool."

It was no more than an hour later that they spotted five bedraggled Apaches from a distance.

Mort was the first to say something. "Uh, Sheriff?"

Mitch nodded. "Stay here," he instructed. He turned southeast to meet the Indians, slowing his horse down to a walk as he neared them to show that he was peaceful. When he was within twenty yards of the men, he recognized one of them as a scout he had ridden with many times.

"Broken Feather." Mitch spoke Apache. Many of the Apache scouts had never learned English.

The Apache's eyes lit up in recognition. "Mitch. I thought we'd never meet again."

"Those were dark days."

Broken Feather inclined his head and looked beyond to Trace and Mort. The question remained unspoken.

"They ride with me," Mitch said.

It was clear from Broken Feather's expression that he didn't trust them. "What brings you this way?"

"I work as the sheriff of a small town to the south. I am tracking three outlaws who have robbed and killed in Tucson."

Broken Feather's smile was bitter. His companions had moved their horses a few yards back, a sign that they realized this was a friendly meeting and they had no reason to be part of it. "So you still work as a scout, tracking white men this time, not Apache."

Mitch returned the smile with one of his own, also bitter. "I am glad that you were able to avoid the Army's effort to move all Apache to a reservation on the other side of this country."

Broken Feather laughed, but there was no humor in it. "There are times I wish I had gone with them. It is a hard life that I have chosen."

"No harder than the life in Florida. I have heard that many of your people died there from starvation and disease."

"At least I would have died with my family," Broken Feather observed with a wry expression. "Your father was Apache, Mitch. You are part of my people. How have you escaped the shame?" Broken Feather practically spit the question out.

"I haven't. When I was first appointed sheriff in Paxton, four miners beat me on the road back to town and left me to die. I had to fight to be accepted."

Broken Feather looked away into the distance. "Why does the white man hate the Apache? I spend my days avoiding contact with loud, greedy white men."

"How do you live out here?"

Broken Feather frowned. "I live out here the same way I have always lived out here, only now I have to be cautious. The men who ride with me want to go to Mexico. They think it will be better down there."

"They may be right."

"It was good to see you again, Mitch."

"And you, Broken Feather." Mitch turned his horse first to head back to Trace and Mort.

"Mitch!"

He turned and Broken Feather pointed northeast. "The men you seek, there were three of them?"

Mitch nodded.

"We saw them. They are a few miles that way." Broken Feather and the others turned their horses around and rode south before Mitch could thank him.

Chapter Ten

Mitch urged his horse on, riding ahead of the others. For all he knew, Trace and Mort had given up and turned around to wait for him back in Hayden.

He wasn't sure what he wanted to do, how to rout the gang. He didn't want to kill them if he could help it—dead bodies on horseback in the hot sun for a day would start to smell bad. He recalled having to kill two wanted men right after he'd been cut loose from the Army. They had entered his camp and drawn their guns, and he'd been forced to kill them. Mitch was too far away from the nearest town, so he had cut off their heads, scooping out the brains and offal and filling the skull cavities with sand. He'd buried the headless bodies in shallow graves in the sand. It had been grisly work.

He doubted that Trace or Mort would be much help if it came down to that in this instance.

As he neared the Hayes gang, they spotted him and

urged their horses into a gallop. Mitch spurred his
horse and went after them. There was no turning back
now, no finding ways to ambush them or falling back
and planning a new way to attack them. He drew his
Colt, ready to return fire.

Pen Hayes shot wildly at Mitch, but it was hard to
draw a bead on a moving target, especially since they
were both moving. Elmer followed suit and so did
Rolly Rollins. As Mitch dodged bullets, all he could
do was return fire. He felt the warmth of a bullet near
his shoulder, but there was no time to find out if he
had been hit.

"Don't come any closer, Sheriff," Pen Hayes called
out. "Take Trace and the others and leave now."

There was no time to find out how he knew the
names of the deputies. "We have to take you and your
brother and Rolly in, Pen," Mitch replied. "Where's the
money?"

There was a flurry of shooting as Trace and Mort
caught up with him and traded shots. Elmer fell from
his horse and lay in the sand. Mitch didn't know if he
was dead or alive, but he didn't think Elmer was going
anywhere real soon. Mort fell back to keep an eye on
the fallen man. Rolly stopped and turned around to fire
another round at them, but Trace caught him square
between the eyes.

"Stay with him," Mitch ordered Trace.

"Why? He's dead," Trace shouted back from his
horse.

"Go back," Mitch ordered once more. "Stay with the
body."

Trace hesitated; then a bullet whined past Mitch and
Trace blinked in surprise, looked down, and saw the

blood on his shoulder. Trace grimaced in pain. Mitch started to slow down. Trace waved him on with his good hand. "Go on. Get the other man. I'm all right. I'll stay here like you ordered." He pulled his horse up short, wheeled around, and headed back to the body.

Pen Hayes, the last of the gang members, had made it into a canyon about a mile from where Trace was shot. Mitch entered cautiously. He listened for the sounds of another horse echoing off the walls and followed the sounds as best he could. After a while, the sounds stopped. Mitch stayed close to one of the canyon walls as he moved stealthily forward. Just as he came to the end of one wall, Pen came out from around the corner and launched himself at Mitch. The two men pitched backward onto the sandy floor of the canyon, Pen getting a couple of surprise punches in. Mitch was dazed and surprised enough for Pen to kick him in the rib cage. Mitch grunted, and when Pen kicked out a second time, Mitch grabbed his leg and pulled Pen down.

Pen rolled away from Mitch and got up quickly. Mitch was still too unsteady to get up fast. As Pen struggled to free his gun from its holster, he came after Mitch again with the toe of his boot. He kicked out at Mitch one more time as he freed his gun. This time, Mitch was ready for him. He grabbed Pen's ankle and pulled him onto the ground. Pen's gun went off, the bullet echoing through the canyon. Pen released his hold on the gun to get a better swing at Mitch. Mitch avoided the blow. Pen tried to scramble away from Mitch and toward his gun, but Mitch cut him off.

Crouched in a fight-or-flight position, Pen turned and ran. Mitch reached for his gun but discovered that he'd lost it in the fight. He picked up Pen's gun and slipped it into his holster so it wouldn't be used against him again.

By this time, Pen had disappeared into the canyon. Mitch left his horse and Pen's in a box canyon and tracked him on foot. The sandy floor made it easy for a while to follow Pen, but eventually the soft sand gave way to rocky floors with light sand that held no tracks.

Canyon walls rose and fell. Pen Hayes could be in a dozen places by now, waiting for Mitch to get tired and leave. Even an expert tracker like Mitch couldn't find a man who was determined to get away from him in here. He was about to turn around and head back to the horses. If he took Pen's horse, he would slow down the outlaw.

It wasn't much, but a few stray grains of sand rained down on his head. Mitch paused, his hand on the gun in his holster. He looked up just as the gun cleared the leather and shot at Pen as he tried to ambush Mitch. Pen fell to the canyon floor with a thud and a groan. Mitch checked his assailant over quickly. His head had been injured in the fall and he was bleeding from his scalp. Mitch helped the outlaw to his feet and escorted him back to the horses.

"Where's the money?" Mitch asked his prisoner.

"Go to hell."

"It'll go easier on you if you give the money back," Mitch explained.

Pen studied him with cold, hard eyes. "You're in on it with the rest of them, aren't you?"

"In on what?" Mitch got no answer. He tried a different tack. "One of my deputies is the fifth Hayes gang member. Which one is it?"

Pen just eyed Mitch, finally breaking into a big grin. "You don't know anythin', do you?"

"What are you talking about?"

Pen chuckled. "You'll find out soon enough."

Mitch led Pen Hayes, hands tied to his saddle, out of the canyon, where Trace and Mort waited with their captives—Rolly was dead and Elmer was still alive but badly injured.

Trace wore a sling for his wounded shoulder. Elmer looked beat up, Mitch thought. But then, he had fallen from his horse after being shot. His leg was bleeding and someone had propped him back up on his horse. Rolly's body was slung over his horse. The air was charged as if heated words had been traded between Elmer and Trace, but Mitch didn't think much of it.

No one spoke until they could see the town of Hayden.

"Say, wasn't there some money from that bank robbery that was never recovered?" Trace asked Mitch. His tone suggested that he had asked this casually, but Mitch suspected that Trace was itching to find the money.

Mitch shrugged. "Yes, but I checked the saddles and I haven't found anything."

Earlier, when the men stopped for a short rest, Mitch had thoroughly checked the saddlebags of the outlaws. A few dollars lay at the bottom of each pouch along with several wanted posters, but there was no bank money to be found.

Mitch had plenty of time to think while they escorted the outlaws to Hayden. Either the outlaws hadn't gone near the place where they'd hidden the money originally, or they did get the money but when they realized they were being followed, they hid it again.

The surviving outlaws were in bad shape by the time they reached Hayden in the early evening. Elmer was sweating from the beginning of an infection in his bullet wound, and Pen kept falling asleep. Mitch had seen that symptom in other men who had taken a great fall, especially if they were knocked on the head. Pen had a great goose egg on the back of his head.

Neither outlaw was talkative on the way back to Hayden.

Before they left Hayden, Mitch had made note of where the undertaker was. Now the information came in handy as he stopped by to drop off Rolly Rollins's body. The undertaker's assistant took the body.

"That'll be five dollars," he said.

Mitch took coins out of Rollins's saddlebag and handed them to the assistant.

"You want a headstone?"

Mitch shook his head. "Just bury him." He turned to Pen and Elmer. "He have any family you know of?"

Neither was in great shape, but Pen managed to speak up. "Nope. Folks are dead. No brothers or sisters."

"Wife or children?"

Elmer spoke up this time. "He was married to a little girl in Denver."

Mitch wasn't sure what to do with Rollins's gear. He resolved to take it back to Paxton, where maybe he could sell it. He'd keep the money in his office until he found Rollins's wife.

"Is there a doctor in town?" Mitch asked the undertaker's assistant.

The assistant eyed the two injured men as though he

was weighing whether to tell Mitch where the doctor was located or offer to take the dying men off his hands. He finally opted to give directions to the doctor's surgery.

Mitch thanked him and escorted the prisoners to the Hayden jail. He brought them inside and looked around for the cell keys. Once he found them, Mitch brought Pen and Elmer Hayes back to the first cell and locked them up.

"Mort, go find a doctor to patch these men up."

Mort ducked his head and went off.

"I'm going to look for Henry," Trace said, then left.

A few minutes after Mort and Trace had left, the mayor of Hayden stopped by the jail while Mitch was making a list of things he needed to do. The mayor turned out to be the owner of the Silver Moon Hotel and owned a large copper mining claim.

"Jack Hayden," he said, offering his hand. Mayor Hayden was short and skinny with sparse sandy hair and a clean-shaven face.

Mitch shook the mayor's hand and introduced himself.

"You're one of the fellas who shot up my hotel." He said it matter-of-factly. It didn't seem to bother him.

"Well, I'm responsible for the men who went in there waving their guns around. I had instructed them to wait until the outlaws had left the hotel. No sense in getting bystanders shot up." Mitch had an idea. "I'm sellin' the gear of the dead man we brought back. I can give you some of that money for the trouble of gettin' your hotel shot up."

Mayor Hayden nodded briefly. " 'Preciate it. I'll just

get someone to patch the holes, but I think a couple of kerosene lanterns were busted as well."

"Go ahead and replace them and send me the bill back in Paxton. I'll make sure you get paid."

"You left one of your deputies behind, I understand."

"In case the gang double-backed," Mitch explained, suddenly very weary. "They did that once before."

The mayor shrugged. "Most of my townsfolk can handle themselves pretty good, but it was good of you to keep a man back here to help protect the town." He seemed to think for a minute, then said, "By the way, I've seen your crew of deputies and some of 'em seem a little—rough. I've heard good things about you, though, Sheriff."

Mitch smiled. "These are men I deputized to go after the Hayes gang."

Mayor Hayden's eyebrows went up. He went over to the jail and took a look at Pen and Elmer Hayes. "Those the boys who broke out of that Tucson jail?"

Mitch nodded.

"Tough place to break out of. Must have had help." The mayor grinned. "They don't look so tough now. Got some lead in 'em."

Mitch nodded. "They put up a fight."

"Good thing you were faster than them. This all of 'em?"

"There were two others, but they're dead. One of them was killed early on when we captured them the first time before the trial."

"And the other one was killed just today?"

"Killed out there. I brought his body back here and left it with the undertaker."

Jack Hayden appeared to think about it for a moment, then nodded. "Well, you do a fine job, Sheriff. If you ever want a job in Hayden, you're welcome here."

"Thank you, Mayor. But it looks like I'll be in Paxton for a long time."

Before the mayor took his leave, Mitch asked him if there was a telegraph office.

"Over at the assayer's office," Hayden replied.

Mitch thought long and hard about the Hayes gang, Trace Beaumont showing up in Paxton when he did, and the extreme amount of interest in the missing bank money that Trace had shown after the Hayes brothers were captured.

Mitch thought about Henry Sturms and his amazing resemblance to a well-known outlaw, who should, by all rights, be dead. And he thought about Mort Keegan, who rode into Paxton with the other two men. Of the three, Mort should seem to be the one to watch out for, but had been less trouble for Mitch than Trace or Henry.

All three men had claimed not to have been together long—more for company on the road since they were going the same way than for any other reason. But none of the men were what they appeared to be. Even Trace, a man he had known when they were growing up, was not being honest with Mitch about his past. But every time Mitch thought he had an answer, it was closely followed by another question.

Mort came back with a doctor following him. Mitch inspected the doctor's bag and took out a few things that could be weapons in the hands of a desperado. Then he took the doctor back to his patients and stayed nearby while the doctor tended to their wounds.

When Trace and Henry came back, Mitch had Mort go back to guard the doctor while he fixed up the prisoners.

"He was sportin'," Trace said. "Little Mexican gal."

Henry grinned.

Mitch hadn't spotted a brothel tent in the town, but that didn't mean there wasn't one.

"You ask those boys about the bank money, Sheriff?" Trace asked.

Mitch avoided answering Trace's question. "Doc's taking care of their injuries right now."

Trace looked restless. "I could use a good meal. Think I'll stroll down to one of the eatin' tents."

Henry joined him. Trace looked back. "Either one of you want to join us?"

"Can't right now," Mitch said. "I have to watch out for the doc."

Trace nodded. "Those boys aren't to be fooled with. You join us when Doc's done. Mort? Are you coming?"

Mort hesitated, appearing to be torn. "Er, I thought I'd stay here in case the sheriff needs me. I'm not hungry, anyway."

Trace looked over at Mitch. "You don't need any help right now, do you, Sheriff?"

Mitch looked from one man to the other. Something was going on here, but he couldn't put his finger on it. "No, I'm fine. Don't you want to stay around and have the doctor look at your wound?"

Trace shrugged, then winced. "I've had worse. Maybe I'll have him look at it later."

"I have a few things to do before I join you."

Mitch was relieved when they were gone. He wasn't

sure what it was, but the behavior of the three men bothered him. He'd be glad when the Hayes brothers were out of his custody and the bank money was found.

He thought about what he ought to do. By rights, he should bring the Hayes brothers back to Tucson, but it was out of the way. He knew a gallows was probably already in place.

The doctor came out of the cell with his black bag. Mitch inspected it to make sure everything came out that had gone in.

"Thanks, Doc." He paid the doctor and when he was once again alone in the office, he wrote up a receipt for the medical attention. Seemed kind of a shame to waste good money since the Hayes brothers would be hanged in a few days, but it wasn't his call to make. Seemed like Trace and Mort had been awfully careful not to kill all of the gang members. And Trace kept asking about the bank money. Made Mitch awfully suspicious, but maybe Trace was just curious about where the money was.

Mitch went back into the cells to check up on Pen and Elmer. "You boys feeling better?"

Elmer was lying on one of the cots, his injured leg with a dressing wrapped around it. Pen had a bandage on his head. They both turned and scowled at Mitch.

"I can see you're better already. Maybe you'd like to tell me where the money is. Won't do you any good from a jail cell."

Elmer closed his eyes and crossed his arms. "Or a gallows. Maybe we can make a deal."

"No deal involves either of you two being released."

"If we offer to split the money with you, Sheriff," Pen said in an agreeable tone. "Two of our gang mem-

112

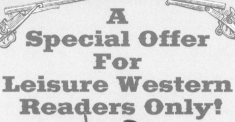

Get Four Books Totally
F R E E* –
A Value between
$16 and $20

Tear here and mail your FREE* book card today!

**PLEASE RUSH
MY FOUR FREE***
**BOOKS TO ME
RIGHT AWAY!**

LeisureWestern Book Club
P.O. Box 6613
Edison, NJ 08818-6613

bers is gone anyways. You can have one of their shares."

"Not interested. I like my job just fine. Being a hunted man the rest of my life don't appeal to me," Mitch said, realizing that neither Hayes brother was aware of how close to being a hunted man Mitch had come.

Pen snarled. "Suit yourself. We'll get out of here before we end up back in Tucson, you can be sure of that."

He said it with such confidence that Mitch wondered what he had missed. He left the cell area and went back to the Hayden sheriff's office to think some more.

He took out the paper he had stuffed in his pocket and spread it out on the desk. It read:

WANTED FOR MURDER AND ROBBERY
HENRY ANTRIM
ALSO KNOWN AS
BILLY THE KID
LAST SEEN IN NEW MEXICO TERRITORY
ANTRIM IS 5' 5",
WITH LIGHT BROWN HAIR,
WITH PROMINENT FRONT TEETH

Mitch frowned. The physical description sounded like Henry Sturms. Trace had been evasive when he confronted his friend about Sturms's identity. But Mitch knew that a lot of men looked like Billy the Kid.

But Mitch had read that Pat Garrett had shot Billy the Kid and he had died that night back in Fort Sumner. At least, that was the story that was circulating. It wouldn't be the first time another man was shot in place of the intended victim. Mitch didn't know Garrett personally, but he'd heard only good reports of Garrett's conduct as a lawman. But even a good lawman could make a mistake.

Mitch wondered about Sturms and about Trace's eagerness to get information on the missing money.

The only man that Mitch hadn't thought much about was Mort Keegan. For a man who hung around Trace and Henry, two men clearly on the other side of the law, he didn't seem to have much of a past.

Mitch wondered about that.

Chapter Eleven

Before Mitch went out for a meal, he stopped by the telegraph office and sent a message to Sheriff MacLean in Tucson, notifying him of the capture of the Hayes brothers.

After that was done, Mitch joined Trace, Mort, and Henry for a meal at the closest tent café, the one with the FOOD sign out front. When they were done, Mort and Henry left to find a saloon, but Mitch and Trace stayed around for a refill of coffee.

"You goin' over to the saloon a little later?" Trace asked.

Mitch shook his head. "I'm stayin' with the prisoners tonight. I'll set you and the others up with a place to stay. You might want to get that bullet wound looked at before too long."

"Yeah, I will. Now, how 'bout that hotel?" Trace asked, standing up.

Mitch shook his head. "Too expensive for county

money. I saw a tent hotel down the street from the jail.
Besides, Mort and Henry seem bound and determined
to spend most of their time in a saloon. Seein' it's
Friday, there'll probably be a lot of sportin' goin' on."

"What do you do for fun, Mitch?"

Mitch smiled and shook his head. "Don't know that
there's a lot of fun in my job, Trace."

"Why don't you go find yourself a nice whore and
take the night off? I'll stay with the prisoners."

"Thanks for the offer, but I don't feel right about it.
It's my responsibility to get those prisoners back to
Tucson, not yours."

Trace was silent for a moment, then said, "I know
you don't trust me or Mort or Henry, and I probably
should have let you know this sooner, but there's usually been another party around."

Mitch waited. Trace looked around, then motioned
to Mitch to follow him outside. Mitch left money on
the table for the meals and stepped outside the tent.

They walked back to the jail and once they were
inside, Trace reached inside his pocket. He showed
Mitch a badge that said "Pinkerton."

Mitch took the badge and inspected it. He raised his
eyebrows. "You're with the Pinkerton Agency?" He
tried to keep the doubt out of his voice.

Trace nodded briefly. "I've been following Elmer
and Pen for the last few months, trying to catch them
and recover money from a previous robbery."

"Where?"

"In New Mexico Territory. Las Cruces."

Mitch hadn't heard of any bank robbery in New
Mexico, but that didn't mean that it didn't happen. He

knew the Hayes gang had worked most of Arizona and New Mexico territory.

Mitch handed the badge back to Trace. "Why didn't you say something to me earlier?"

Trace shrugged. "I wasn't sure who to trust. There's always been someone around."

"I guess I can see that." Mitch still wasn't sure what to think of a Pinkerton man who didn't let a lawman know who he was up front. He hadn't had all that much experience with Pinkerton, so he wasn't sure how they operated. It didn't seem right that a Pinkerton wouldn't come to the law in town.

"That's why I've been asking all those questions about the money."

"Sure." It would explain why Pen and Elmer seemed to know Trace, but it didn't explain why they hadn't been open about knowing him.

Trace was pacing back and forth across the small office. "So you'll tell me if you find the money, won't you?"

"Of course," Mitch said. "Are the other two men with you also with Pinkerton?"

Trace stopped pacing. "Mort and Henry?" He looked a little confused. "Oh, I see what you mean. No, they don't know I'm with the agency. I suspect that either Henry or Mort is the fifth member of the gang."

"How long have you known them?"

"Not long. They both seemed to have a reason for going after the Hayes gang, so I offered to go in with them."

"They don't seem to like each other much. It's almost as if they didn't know each other before traveling with you."

117

Trace nodded. "Yes, I find that strange as well."

"Now why don't we get you and the others beds at that tent hotel nearby?"

After paying for three beds and sending Trace to tell the others, Mitch went back to the jailhouse. There was a cot in the corner for the sheriff or deputy to use if he had to stay overnight. It was comfortable enough after he'd laid down his bedroll, but Mitch still couldn't sleep.

He'd left the door to the cell area slightly ajar in case one of the men called out for something in the night. Sometime late at night, he woke from a light, troubled sleep to listen to the two prisoners talking in low voices. He sat up and concentrated on their exchange.

"You think we can convince him to break us out of here?" one of the Hayes brothers asked.

"We know where the money is. If he wants a share, he'll have to get us out of here."

"You sayin' we promise him a share?"

"Yeah, and we pay him, all right. In lead."

Mitch waited, hoping they would reveal the name— was it Trace? Mort? Henry? But the Hayes brothers had fallen silent. Mitch fell back into his light sleep, tossing and turning for the rest of the night with dreams of chasing the Hayes brothers through the burning fires of hell with the devil in the background, laughing.

The next morning, Trace stopped by before breakfast.

Mitch was already up and had splashed his face with water.

"Went to see the doctor like you suggested." He held up the new sling.

118

"You'll be paid back for the doctor." Mitch went over to the desk and wrote down a note to include Trace's doctor visit in his pay.

"Did you learn anything more from the prisoners last night?" Trace asked Mitch.

"No." Mitch rolled up his bedroll. He figured he had no obligation to reveal what he'd learned from the prisoners the night before. Besides, Trace's confession that he was a Pinkerton didn't stop Mitch from distrusting Trace. "I need to go out for a little while. I have to see if there's a message for me from the sheriff in Tucson. Can you see to breakfast for the prisoners?"

Trace grinned. "Of course. I'll need the keys to the cell so I can give them their meals."

Mitch thought about the conversation that he overheard last night. "You don't need to open the cells. There are slots to slip the meals through. And let's lock up your guns. Don't want any accidents," Mitch said, "especially as how you only have one good hand for a while."

Trace reluctantly handed over his guns and Mitch locked them in the lock box.

"But what about coffee?"

"They get water and you can put it in a shallow bowl. I don't want them throwing scalding coffee on an officer of the law and escaping." Sheriff MacLean had told Mitch about his early years as a law enforcer, and that was one of the tricks prisoners used sometimes.

Trace nodded. "All right. If I'm not here when you get back, I've gone for breakfast. Are we bringing the prisoners to Tucson, or back to Paxton?"

"I'm going to find that out right now," Mitch said,

keeping his impatience in check. He left Trace in charge of the prisoners.

The assayer had just opened up for business. When Mitch asked about any telegrams for him, the assayer went back to his desk and brought a piece of paper back.

"It came in late last night. I almost missed it," the assayer told him.

Mitch thanked him and went outside to read it.

> *Will send deputies to pick up prisoners tomorrow*
>   *Sheriff MacLean*

Mitch figured that if the deputies had left early in the morning, they'd be coming into town soon. He decided to go get breakfast at one of the tent cafés.

While he was waiting for his bacon and eggs, he thought some more about what he'd heard the Hayes brothers talk about last night. One of his men might betray him. Maybe Trace was a Pinkerton, but Mitch needed more proof than a badge. A man could get a badge off a dead man. And it wasn't uncommon for men to go to work for the law, then find out it pays better on the other side of the law. A Pinkerton badge would come in real handy if you wanted to get another man's trust.

When he was finished with his coffee and plate of eggs and bacon and fried bread, he walked back to the jail. Trace must have gone for breakfast just as he'd said earlier because only the Hayes brothers were in the jailhouse. And they weren't going anywhere soon.

"You get fed?" he asked.

"Your man give us some eggs and bread." Pen glared at him. "Could use some coffee."

Mitch smiled. "Maybe the deputies from Tucson will oblige you when they get here. Do you know one of my deputies from somewhere else?"

"Why do you ask?" Pen sneered.

"I heard you talking last night, and you seemed to know one of them. You were talking about someone helping you escape."

"If it was the one who was just here, would we still be here?" Pen asked in a sarcastic tone.

"So it's the other man?" Mitch said casually.

"If it was, would he have shot at us from the window of the hotel when we escaped the other day?" Elmer asked.

"Why should we tell you? Maybe we still have a chance of escaping." Pen grinned.

"Is one of my deputies the fifth member of your gang?"

Elmer laughed. "We're not telling you anything."

Pen joined him and said to his brother, "Let him worry."

A man with a badge came through the front door. Mitch recognized him as one of the members of the Tucson posse a few weeks ago. "Deputy Aguillera," he said, shaking Mitch's hand, clearly recognizing him as well.

The deputy stepped up to the cells to inspect his prisoners. "They don't look so good."

"Lead poisoning can do that to you."

Deputy Aguillera shrugged and smiled. "It won't make no difference soon anyway. They're scheduled to swing day after tomorrow."

"Did you come alone?"

"No, my partner is getting us some coffee."

"Hey, Deputy," Pen called out, "how 'bout gettin' us some coffee, too? This half-breed sheriff won't give us any."

The deputy looked questioningly at Mitch. "Sheriff MacLean once told me that a prisoner threw hot coffee at him and tried to grab his gun," Mitch explained. "Since then, I don't give dangerous prisoners anything that might be used as a weapon."

Aguillera nodded in understanding. "I think he told me that story once. Good thing to remember."

A younger deputy came inside with two mugs of coffee in one hand.

"That's Deputy Frank," Aguillera said.

Mitch nodded to the younger man.

"You ride all night?" Mitch asked.

Aguillera shook his head. "We bedded down for a time." He took the coffee the other deputy offered him and sipped it.

Trace and Henry arrived.

"Where's Mort?" Mitch asked.

Henry looked at Trace and Trace at Henry. "I haven't seen him since last night," Trace told Mitch.

"He wasn't in his bed this morning when I woke up," Henry added. "In fact, his bed didn't look as if he'd slept in it."

"He told me last night that he was goin' sportin'," Trace added.

Mitch nodded, then turned his attention back to Deputy Aguillera. He handed the keys to the cell to the deputy. "I'm glad you're taking them back from here."

Aguillera nodded. "Any chance you found the

money they stole from the Tucson bank?"

Mitch shook his head. "Not yet. But it can't be far."

The other deputy made a face. "Sons of bitches took my money. I had my life savings in that bank."

Aguillera looked at his young partner calmly. "I keep telling you, Frank, you need to keep your money in your mattress or, better yet, put it in a jar and bury it on your property. Banks are nothing but trouble."

Mitch addressed Trace. "Why don't you go looking for Mort. We'll be heading back to Paxton soon." He turned to Henry. "Go get the horses ready to transport the prisoners."

When his two men had gone, he sat down with the Tucson deputies. "I don't know what's going on, but one of the men riding with me has been asking an awful lot of questions. Claims to be with Pinkerton."

"You think he could be?" Frank asked.

"He showed me a badge, but I've never seen a Pinkerton badge before so I don't know if it's real."

Aguillera frowned. "You need anything?"

Mitch thought a while, then said, "Yes. When you get back to Tucson, could you have the sheriff check on a few things for me?" He outlined what he wanted and Aguillera agreed, writing down the information to ask the sheriff when they got back to Tucson.

"You'll be back in Paxton by tomorrow? The sheriff can check on this and send a telegram."

Mitch confirmed that he would, then went to open the cell and escort Elmer and Pen Hayes out. The doctor had left a crutch for Elmer to use with his game leg.

"Well, Pen, looks like you were finally lookin' at the wrong end of the gun," Aguillera said cheerily.

Pen glared at the deputies. Frank reached out and took the crutch away from Elmer. "We don't want you hurting yourself, Elmer."

Mitch turned to the deputies. "I have to check on a couple of things. Tell Trace and Henry to wait for me back here. And Mort, if he shows up."

The deputies thanked him and Mitch left.

It was only a glimmer of an idea, but Mitch thought it was worth looking into. He headed over to the Silver Moon Hotel. The same young man from yesterday was manning the front desk. Mitch doubted the boy had started shaving yet.

Mitch frowned. "Did you rent that room out last night?"

"As a matter of fact, I did. To one of the fellows who came in with you after those men."

Mitch described Mort. The clerk confirmed that that was the man who rented the room.

"Is he still here?"

The clerk looked behind him at the board that held the room keys. "I haven't seen him leave and the key is still gone from my board."

Mitch went up to the room and knocked on the door. No one answered. He tried the door, which opened easily. The smell of a dying man releasing his bowels permeated the room.

Mort's body was sprawled facedown in the center of the room. Mitch went over and inspected the body. Mort's throat had been cut. His gun was still in its holster so he hadn't been expecting his death. Mitch knew a little about death and what it did to a body. Mort had died sometime last night.

Mitch took the time to look at the room itself. Someone, Mort or the killer, had torn the room apart. The mattress was ripped up one side and down the other and the dresser drawers had been taken out. Someone had tried to prise up a couple of the floorboards. In fact, there was a hole in the east corner of the room where the floorboards had been removed. It was clear that someone else had the idea that the money might have been here and Mort had surprised the killer.

It had been a quiet death, and Mitch wondered what Mort had thought at the last. He still had no clear idea of Mort's past or what reason he had to hook up with Trace Beaumont and Henry Sturms.

With no more to go on than that, Mitch left the room and went back to the clerk.

"The man was killed in that room sometime last night." The clerk's eyes widened. "Please go back there and lock the door. Don't let anyone into the room until I bring the mayor, the doctor, and the undertaker back here."

"Yes, sir," the clerk said, reaching in back of him to get the other copy of the room key.

Mitch left and went down to the mayor's office. Jack Hayden was in. Mitch told him what he had discovered. Hayden's eyebrows raised. "Murder? Was it one of the Hayes brothers?"

Mitch shook his head. "They were locked up all night. I just wanted you to know about the death."

"You'll stay to investigate, won't you?"

Mitch paused to think, then said, "Mayor Hayden, this is a job for Sheriff MacLean and his men. I left two of his deputies back at the jailhouse. I'll try to catch them before I leave. I have doubts about the innocence of my own men, so I'll be asking some questions to clear them or to further investigate. But I need to get back to Paxton by Friday. One thing I know for sure is that whoever killed Mort was after the missing bank money, and he may have found it."

The mayor nodded. Mitch had an idea. He excused himself and went back to the hotel. The clerk was still behind the desk.

"Do you have a safe for your customers to keep valuables?"

The clerk hesitated, then nodded. "We just got it a few months ago."

"The three men who rented the room where the shootout happened yesterday," Mitch began, "did they leave anything with you to put in a safe?"

Again there was a pause, then the clerk said, "They didn't look like they had two coins to rub together, Sheriff, but it's possible. I didn't check them in. Tim did."

"Open your safe and bring me what they left behind."

The clerk disappeared into a small room behind the desk. He reappeared a few minutes later with a bundle wrapped in dirty bandannas.

Mitch took the bundle and examined it. Opening a corner of it revealed the money the Hayes gang had robbed from the bank in Tucson. He handed the packet back to the clerk.

"Please put this back in the safe. I'm going to talk to Mayor Hayden."

He went back down the hall. The mayor stood outside the room. He told the mayor what the clerk had found in the safe.

"Can you take care of this while I try to catch the

deputies before they leave town?" he asked Mayor Hayden.

"I'll get a couple of men to clean up and let the undertaker know about this body. I'll have to telegraph Sheriff MacLean and he'll send a couple of men up here to investigate."

"If the deputies from Tucson are still at the jail with the prisoners, I'll let them know about the murder. And there's one more thing I think you should know."

"What do you plan to do with the money?" Hayden asked.

"I'll let the deputies know about it and they'll take care of it. If they've left already, you can turn it over to whoever comes here to investigate."

Back at the jail, Henry and Trace were waiting.

"Where are the deputies?" Mitch asked.

"They needed to get the prisoners back to Tucson for the hanging," Henry said. "They left a few minutes ago."

"Did you find Mort?" Trace asked.

"I'll tell you when I get back." Mitch went back outside and commandeered a saddled horse from in front of the general store across the street.

He headed in the direction the deputies would have gone, and because they were going slower than he was, he was able to catch up to them within five minutes.

"Sheriff," Aguillera greeted him, looking surprised, "what is it?"

"One of my deputies was found dead in the Silver Moon Hotel. His throat was cut."

Aguillera turned to Frank. "We need to go back."

The lawmen and their prisoners headed back to the jailhouse. Trace and Henry were still there.

Trace asked first. "Mitch, what is it? Why are the deputies back?"

"I found Mort Keegan at the Silver Moon Hotel. He's dead. His throat's been cut."

"Probably some whore killed him," Trace said.

"He had checked into the same hotel room that the Hayes brothers had stayed in. Looked like Mort or the killer thought the money was hidden in the room."

Henry was chewing on a sliver of wood. He switched it from one side of his mouth to the other. "What do we do?" he asked.

"You stay here and watch the prisoners. Make sure the Hayes brothers aren't disturbed." The deputies had installed the brothers back in the jail cell.

"What do you plan to do?" Henry asked.

"Ask some questions. Deputy Aguillera will help me question people. Deputy Frank will stay here with you."

Trace and Henry looked at each other. "Maybe you should let me help you with the questioning," Trace offered. "I've had some experience."

"Thanks, but no."

"Why not? You've seen my badge."

Even Deputy Aguillera was looking at Mitch, curiosity on his face.

"Because you're a suspect."

Anger crossed Trace's face. "And you're not?"

Mitch shrugged. "I didn't know him very well. I only met him a few days ago. You knew him. Both of you."

"I hardly knew him either," Henry protested. "I had no reason to kill him."

Trace didn't say anything, but he caught Mitch's eye and said to Henry, "What he means is that Mort was in the room where you and I caught the Hayes brothers. He must have been looking for the money from the Tucson bank robbery. Someone else had the same idea and came in, surprised him, and killed him."

"So?" Henry said, "That someone could have been the good sheriff here."

Trace shook his head. "No. Mort didn't know Mitch well enough to trust him. He wouldn't have turned his back on him. But he might have turned his back on you or me."

Chapter Twelve

Mitch went to the tent hotel and the deputy asked around at the saloons. Mitch wanted to establish Trace's alibi and Henry's before he went looking elsewhere for Mort's killer. He interviewed the owner of the tent hotel and several other guests. All of them verified that Henry and Trace had been in the tent hotel by midnight.

It wasn't a great alibi, but from the condition of the body, Mitch was pretty certain that Mort died sometime after midnight.

He went back to the Silver Moon Hotel to talk to the young clerk. He ran into the men who were taking the body out of the hotel through the side door. The mayor and the doctor spotted him and came over.

"Doc, you have a notion of when the man was killed?" Mitch asked.

The doctor, a tall, burly man who looked as though he should be cutting wood rather than treating patients, frowned and rubbed the back of his neck. "Near as I can tell from the condition of the body, he had to have been killed after eleven, maybe even after midnight. It was moderately cool last night, so there wasn't much deterioration."

Mitch thanked the doctor, then turned to the mayor and told him that he'd notified the Tucson deputies and they were helping with the investigation.

"Thank you, Sheriff. Is there anything I can do?"

"Send a telegram to Sheriff MacLean to let him know about the murder. He'll wonder why his deputies haven't come back before now." Mitch turned to the young clerk, who was swallowing so hard his Adam's apple bobbed up and down like a bouncing ball. "Did you notice anyone come in asking for the victim last night?"

"I—I wasn't on duty last night," the young man said. "Tim was on duty." Tim lived in a room at the back of the hotel, the clerk explained. He came out from behind the desk and took Mitch to the room. After the day clerk left, Mitch pounded on the door.

A few moments passed before a bleary-eyed young man opened the door. Mitch announced who he was and what had happened.

Tim opened the door wider and rubbed his eyes to wipe the sleep from them. "Last night? Let me think. I knew who all the renters were—a couple of drummers, a couple staying here until the next stagecoach arrives heading back East, and that circuit preacher, Reverend Wesslund. And the man who was killed, of course."

"Did he bring anyone back to the room?"

Tim thought for a minute, then shook his head. "I don't recall."

"I'm going to describe a couple of men. See if the description helps at all." Mitch described Trace Beaumont and Henry Sturms.

Tim was concentrating hard now, but to no avail. He finally shook his head. "Neither description sounds familiar."

"Were you at the desk the entire evening?"

"I had to go out back a few times to relieve myself or to get some coffee, but that was all. I was at the desk when Mr. Keegan came through the lobby." He yawned. "Are you done? I need my sleep. I'm on duty tonight."

"One more question. When you checked three men into the same room the other day, did they leave a package with you?"

Mitch couldn't be sure, but he thought the color drained from Tim's face.

"Why do you ask?" Tim asked.

"Just answer the question."

He was slow to answer, but finally he said, "I think so. I can't be sure."

Mitch thanked him and left.

He met up with Deputy Aguillera, who told him that descriptions of Trace and Henry were recognized at a couple of saloons last night by the saloon keepers and a few regulars. To the best of his ability, he was able to trace their movements for most of the night.

"So my deputies seem to be in the clear," Mitch said.

Deputy Aguillera nodded. "Why don't you go back to Paxton with your men and I'll keep asking questions around here for a few more hours."

Mitch thanked him and told him where the bank money could be picked up. The deputy promised to get Mitch's message to Sheriff MacLean.

When Mitch got back to the jailhouse, Henry was nervously pacing the floor and Trace was seated with the other deputy, quietly talking.

Frank, the other deputy, looked up. "Hi, Sheriff, any luck?"

Aguillera came in. "I talked to several of the saloon keepers who were able to place Trace at a card game last night till almost midnight. He only left the game to get another whiskey." The deputy looked over at Henry. "And he was either drinking at the same saloon or with one of the saloon girls in her room out back. She confirms it, and so do three other men he tried to pick a fight with."

Henry looked sheepish.

Mitch told the deputy about Tim, the night clerk. "I think he's hiding something—either the fact that he saw the killer or the fact that he took the bank money and hid it in the hotel safe, or maybe both. I'll leave the investigation in your hands."

Aguillera and Mitch shook hands.

"These two are cleared, at least for the moment," Aguillera said. "Make sure they stay around Paxton until we finish our investigation."

Mitch looked at Trace and Henry. "You heard him."

The two men got up. Mitch waited a few moments before adding, "By the way, I found the bank money. The deputies will be taking care of it from here on." He watched their reaction carefully. Both Trace and Henry were good at covering up their disappointment, but not good enough. A look passed between the two temporary deputies.

Trace was the first one to recover. "Well, Sheriff, let's get back to Paxton. I'm sure you have lots to do back there."

It was late morning of the next day when the three men rode into Paxton. Trace and Henry went over to one of the hotels to pay for a room. Mitch went over to his office to see how his deputy was faring.

Alky was propped up outside the jailhouse, his crutch beside him, quietly snoozing.

Mitch kicked his good foot to wake him. Alky woke with a snort.

"Huh? Mitch? You back already?"

"Got the Hayes brothers. Rolly Rollins took a bullet in the head. Elmer took a bullet in the leg. Pen Hayes's head was bandaged. We had to wait for the deputies from Tucson to come pick up their prisoners."

Alky struggled up. "I could use a drink. Coffee, I think."

They walked over to Ellie's Eat Here. Mitch was glad to be back. He knew he should go tell Reid he was back, but he didn't feel like it right away. He had a few things to do.

Mitch told his deputy almost everything that had happened.

"Damn, Sheriff. What are you going to do?" Alky asked.

Mitch thought about it. "Who would I go to for information on Pinkerton agents?"

Alky thought about it. "There has to be a Pinkerton agency in Denver."

Mitch went over to the general store and sent a telegram to the sheriff in Denver. Then he decided to pay a visit to J. Paxton Reid.

Reid was in his office, going over some papers. Jewel was not in the outer office.

He looked up when Mitch entered. "You're back. Was your trip successful?"

Mitch gave him an account of what had gone on.

"Glad to hear the Hayes boys aren't at large anymore." He looked a little more interested in what Mitch had to say about Mort Keegan's murder.

"It had to be a coincidence, Mitch. Why would one of your temporary deputies kill him?"

"If they wanted the bank money."

"How can you be sure the man who killed Mort Keegan, if it's one of those other two men, won't leave town?"

"Greed. He wants the money."

Reid sat back in his chair. "Well, I can't believe that Trace Beaumont has anything to do with it. You yourself told me he was a Pinkerton man."

"He did show me a badge," Mitch said.

"It has to be that other man. Or maybe someone else back in Hayden."

Mitch shrugged.

"I wouldn't like to think I invited a killer to my table," Reid said.

Mitch tried not to show surprise. "You invited Trace to dinner?"

Reid beamed. "I like to think if he tastes Jewel's cooking, he might be interested in staying around." Mitch was well aware that Reid did not approve of his friendship with Jewel, and he was always trying to set her up with other men.

Mitch got up. He handed Reid the receipts for what he paid out, then made his excuses and left. Mitch wasn't sure what he thought of Trace Beaumont having dinner with Reid and his daughter. Jewel had a mind of her own, and her father couldn't bully her into liking a man she didn't care for.

When he was outside, he headed back to his office. Jewel was there with Alky.

"Alky was just telling me you got back a little while ago," she said, smiling.

Mitch nodded and went around his desk to sit in the chair. "Looks like Paxton did all right without me here."

"Oh, it'll get wild tonight, then there's the social tomorrow."

Mitch had forgotten about it, but he didn't let on. He nodded again and looked away to study a wanted poster on his desk.

"I understand you're having company for dinner tonight."

He could see her face light up with delight. "Are you trying to get yourself invited to dinner?"

Mitch looked up. "Your father just told me that he invited Trace Beaumont to dinner."

Jewel frowned. "You're not jealous, are you?"

Mitch shrugged. "Of course not. I just thought you knew. Why should I be jealous? You and I are just friends."

He went back to studying the poster. He wasn't really seeing it, but he wanted to make it clear to Jewel that she didn't have to be beholden to him.

When he looked up again, Jewel's frown deepened. "Huh!"

"What?"

"You aren't jealous!" She turned around and stomped out the door.

Mitch looked at Alky, who wore a puzzled expression that probably mirrored his own.

Alky shook his head. "Women."

Mitch nodded in agreement.

Friday night was always a busy time for Mitch and his deputy. Miners came to town to let off a little steam, and the saloons and dance halls were full.

Mitch hadn't seen Trace or Henry since they arrived in town earlier that day. But after dinner, Mitch was patrolling Main Street when he walked past Trace and Jewel.

Jewel wore her Sunday dress, a light blue calico dress with a white lace collar. She had a deep blue lace shawl draped over her shoulders against the cool night air. Her hair was pinned up with hair combs. Trace's hand rested lightly on her elbow as they talked and strolled. He had cleaned up considerably from being on the road. Mitch imagined that Trace must have spent the better part of the day scrubbing the dirt from underneath his fingernails and he had even donned clean clothes.

Piano music drifted out from one of the saloons. Mitch took up a position down the street from one of the saloons to watch it. He leaned up against a post in front of the assayer's office. He decided to leave Jewel and Trace alone. It wasn't any of his business if they were keeping company.

Trace noticed Mitch first.

"Evenin', Sheriff."

137

"Trace." Mitch nodded in response.

Jewel had been avoiding eye contact until now. She gave him a big smile. "Good to see you're on duty, Mitch."

"We just came from Miss Jewel's house. She cooks like an angel," Trace told Mitch.

Trace tried to pull Jewel closer to him, but Mitch noted with some satisfaction that she seemed to draw slightly away and then crossed her arms as if she was cold instead of guarded.

Mitch didn't say anything.

"I am looking forward to the social on Sunday," Trace continued. "I think I'll be competition for you when Miss Jewel's box lunch comes up for auction."

Mitch smiled. "The money goes to the church fund. The Tucson deputies should be finishing their investigation of Mort Keegan's death soon. You should be able to move on by Monday or Tuesday."

"That was such terrible news," Jewel said. "You found him, didn't you, Mitch?"

Mitch nodded. "Yes."

"I didn't know the man, but it must have been hard on Trace to know that his friend had died so violently." She looked up at Trace. "Trace has been telling me that he's with the Pinkerton Agency. He's thinking of staying around here, maybe making Paxton his home."

Mitch turned to Trace. "Is that so? I thought you had business in Tucson." Tight-lipped about it until now, Trace was suddenly awfully free with the information that he was with the Pinkertons.

The other man shrugged. "Well, now, you know as well as I do that I thought I'd be gone by now, but plans have changed. I've talked to Miss Jewel about staying around here, or at least coming back here once I have finished up my business in Tucson. There's no hurry in it, though. With Keegan's death, I've had to rearrange my plans, and I'm making the best of it." He changed the subject swiftly. "For instance, I am looking forward to the social tomorrow, and Miss Jewel's box lunch sounds tempting, especially with the company that would go with the box lunch." He eyed Jewel the way a wolf eyed a sheep before making it his dinner.

Mitch didn't like the insolence in his look, and he didn't trust Trace's stories about being a Pinkerton man. There was something phony about the whole scene. It probably didn't help Mitch's thoughts when he saw Jewel smile back at Trace with a warmth she had previously reserved only for Mitch.

Mitch took a deep breath and pushed off the post he'd been holding up.

"Where's Henry?"

Trace shook his head. "I haven't seen him since we got into town earlier today. Probably in a saloon, shaking the dust of the road off his boots."

"I'd like both of you to stop by my office tomorrow morning to check in with me."

A dark look crossed Trace's face, but he covered it quickly with a smile. Not quickly enough. "Why, certainly, Sheriff." He touched the brim of his hat. "Now, if you don't mind, I think I'll treat Miss Jewel here to one of those new sparkling drinks."

Mitch touched the brim of his hat to both of them and walked off to make the rounds of saloons and Fanny Belle's whorehouse. He wondered if Madge was free tonight.

Chapter Thirteen

Mitch broke up half a dozen fights after encountering Trace and Jewel that night. Two fights were over cards, three were over saloon girls, and one was just because one drunk accidentally bumped into another drunk, then started shooting up the Bad Dog.

Back in the jailhouse, Mitch was just locking up the last of the drunks when Alky came in, escorting another young man that turned out to be Henry. Alky sat Henry down in one of the chairs in Mitch's office.

"You can figure out what to do with him," Alky said.

"He try to cut another woman?"

Alky shook his head. He'd stopped using the crutch, but was still limping slightly. He put Henry's gun on the desk. "Some drunk insulted his mother."

"No one insults my mother," Henry mumbled. His head was down and when he looked up, his eyes were an icy gray. He reeked of liquor.

"At least he'll be accounted for tomorrow," Mitch said.

Henry roused himself enough to realize where he was. "Say, Sheriff, you're not gonna hold me here, are you?"

"Just till the liquor wears off, Henry."

"I'll be out by Monday, won't I?"

"You thinkin' of goin' someplace?"

Henry's eyes shifted. "Maybe. Depends on a lot of things."

Mitch knew that sometimes drunk men would tell him things they wouldn't tell him when they were sober.

"Say, Henry, did you know that you look a lot like Billy the Kid?"

Henry's eyelids fluttered and he lifted his head in Mitch's direction. He grinned and laughed. "Yeah, that's me, Billy the Kid."

"Did you kill Mort Keegan?"

Henry seemed to sober up a bit. "You tryin' to get a confession from me?" He looked wary and a little crazy, as if he wanted to start a fight. The problem was that he was in no position to fight with Mitch, and somewhere deep down beyond the drink he'd poured into himself, Henry knew it. His shoulders slumped. He got up and shuffled into an empty cell. "I hardly knew Mort Keegan. Kept to hisself. Seemed too good for everyone else. Why'd you ask me anyway? Thought you asked around Hayden an' I was cleared."

"Yeah, I already asked around Hayden and you weren't seen coming in or going out of the hotel that night. And there were several men who were in your company that night when you made the round of saloons and saloon girls. Then a couple of men saw you later at the tent hotel." Mitch shut the cell door and locked it. "But it never hurts to ask a man when he's drunk. He's more likely to tell the truth than when he's sober."

As he left the cell area, he heard Henry mutter, "Billy the Kid. Huh!" Then he joined in the chorus of snoring going on around him—all the drunks sleeping off their binges.

When Mitch came back into the office, he sat on the other chair across from Alky, who had propped his leg up on a stool.

"Busy night."

Mitch nodded. "How many fights you have to bust up?"

Alky shook his head, scratched his beard. "A few. I saw Miss Jewel with your friend."

"He's not my friend," Mitch replied mildly. "He's someone I grew up with, but we weren't really friends."

"He talked to me for a while, told me he saved your life."

Mitch nodded. "He did save me from drowning once. I'd gone in the swimming hole alone and was out in the middle of it when I got a cramp. I couldn't breathe, and I damn near went under. Trace was walking by. He jumped in and pulled me to safety."

"You don't like him, do you?"

Mitch shrugged. "I don't know about that. I think I don't trust him. Too silver-tongued."

"You think he's really a Pinkerton agent?"

Mitch looked away. "That's why I sent a telegram

to the Denver sheriff's office. I asked them to get in touch with the Pinkerton office there and ask about Trace."

They fell silent for a time. Then Alky spoke up again. "You think Miss Jewel really likes him or is she just payin' attention to him to get at you?"

They looked at each other and grinned.

"I gotta go check on Fanny Belle's," Alky said. He got up from his chair. "Gotta make sure there aren't any suspicious characters 'round there."

"The only suspicious character at Fanny Belle's will be you, Alky," Mitch said.

"Bah!" The deputy limped out of the jailhouse.

Mitch got very little sleep. He kept thinking of Jewel with Trace and not liking it much. He didn't like the idea of Trace staying on here either.

Early Saturday morning, he splashed his face with water, then went to Ellie's Eat Here café to order breakfasts for the prisoners. He sat down and had his own meal first.

Reid came into the café, neatly dressed and ready for a day of business. Jewel followed him in as well. They saw Mitch sitting by himself and joined him.

"Good morning, Sheriff," Reid said.

"Morning, Mr. Reid." Mitch nodded to Jewel and stood and pulled a chair out for her. "I hope you had a good evening, Jewel."

She smiled. "Yes, I had a wonderful evening. Trace has asked to take me out to dinner tonight as payment for dinner last night."

Reid was beaming. "It looks like Mr. Beaumont has quite an interest in my daughter."

Mitch nodded. "That's just fine. She deserves the best."

Out of the corner of his eye, he thought Jewel's smile faltered slightly. He tried to put it out of his mind. Ellie placed his breakfast in front of him, filled all three cups with steaming coffee, and took orders for Reid and Jewel.

"Where is he taking your daughter tonight?" Mitch asked Reid.

"Why, I believe there's a dance at the old livery stable," Reid replied.

There were a few dance halls, known as hurdy-gurdies, in Paxton, but a respectable lady wasn't allowed in them. The dance hall girls were paid good money to get the miners to buy drinks and spend their money. As a remedy for the "evils of hurdy-gurdies," as the Reverend Mr. Wesslund called it, some of the more respectable citizens of Paxton would hold chaperoned dances. With the circuit preacher coming to town for a sermon and a social on Sunday, a dance had been hastily organized with local musicians. Lemonade was the drink of choice. No liquor was allowed, and if a man decided to visit a saloon to get his fill of liquor beforehand, he was not allowed into the dance.

With the Temperance Union constantly looming over the saloon business, it was only a matter of time before the majority of townspeople, with the help of the clergy and women with families to look after, would begin to clean up towns out west. Do-gooders who would tout these places as the root of all evil would sweep saloons and hurdy-gurdy halls out of town.

"I *am* sitting at the same table, you know," Jewel

said in an acid-filled tone. "You could just ask me, Mitch."

"Sorry, Jewel." But he didn't think he was sorry. He'd meant to ask Reid in front of Jewel so she'd know it didn't matter to him. He turned back to Reid. "I need to pay the men who went after the Hayes gang with me."

Reid nodded. "Stop by my office later this morning and I'll give you the money to pay them."

When Mitch was finished with his meal, he brought the prisoners' meals back to the jailhouse. Alky had gone back to his room to rest up for the long Saturday night ahead.

Mitch spent the rest of the morning finishing up paperwork. When he was done, he made a list that included everything that had happened to recover the bank money and the Hayes gang, everything that had led up to Mort Keegan being murdered.

Hayes gang captured
Bank money never recovered
Trace Beaumont shows up in Paxton with Mort and Henry
Hayes gang escapes, heading north
Posse catches up to them in Hayden
Captured outside of Hayden
Still no money found
Mort Keegan murdered next day in Hayden hotel
Trace reveals he's with Pinkerton
Money recovered in hotel safe

The order of the happenings bothered him. Trace hadn't showed him a Pinkerton badge before then. He should have waved it around before they went after the Hayeses. Mitch thought about it some more, then realized why it bothered him. Trace had shown him the badge *before* Mort was murdered. He switched the order.

But there was still something wrong. Mitch had checked through his wanted posters and hadn't come up with any outlaw who resembled Mort Keegan. He had come up with plenty of outlaws who matched Trace's description or Henry's, but none who might have been Keegan. He remained an ordinary man who was caught up in unusual circumstances.

By late morning, Abner stopped by the jail with a telegram for Mitch that read:

STILL WORKING ON PINKERTON STOP SHOULD KNOW TOMORROW STOP ARRESTED NIGHT CLERK FOR MURDER STOP SHERIFF MacLEAN

It was a logical conclusion that Tim, the night clerk at the hotel, had killed Mort Keegan. Still, Tim didn't strike Mitch as a killer.

Mitch made another list, trying to figure out the order of events. He tried several times, shuffling the order until he came up with one that seemed likely:

Mort searches room
Finds money
Clerk comes in
Kills Mort
Hides money in safe

Mitch suspected that Tim might have scared off the killer and found the money. He probably wasn't even sure what to do with it, which was why it had been in the hotel safe.

But it still made no sense to Mitch. He thought back to the hotel clerk. Tim hadn't acted as if he had something to hide. So if he did murder Mort Keegan, the only reason would have been for the money from the bank robbery. But Mitch would have thought the clerk would dispose of the body, try to draw attention away from the hotel. On the other hand, the hotel room was all but demolished in an attempt to find the loot.

But it still didn't make any sense. If the clerk found Mort with the money and killed him, why would he hide it in the hotel safe, knowing that the law was in town and might ask him to open the safe? He decided to think about it some more, but in the meantime, Mitch let the prisoners out of their cells. He figured most of the men were sorry enough with the hangovers they had.

Henry was one of the last men to get out.

"I want you to get Trace and come back here," Mitch said. "I have some news about Mort's death."

Henry's eyes widened. "Can I get my gun back?"

Mitch nodded. "You get Trace here, then I'll give you your gun."

"Don't feel right goin' out there without my gun," Henry muttered as he left.

Mitch rolled a cigarette and smoked it. By the time he was finished, Henry was back with Trace.

"Morning, Sheriff," Trace said. He was a little rumpled—clearly having been interrupted in the middle of getting ready for the day. His expression betrayed his impatience. "What's the matter?"

"Just wanted you and Henry to know that you've been cleared of the murder."

Trace's face cleared. "How 'bout that? Well, I knew I didn't do it, but I wasn't sure about Henry here." He clapped Henry on the back to show it was a joke, but Henry returned the favor with a glare.

"You're both free to leave whenever you want to." Mitch handed Henry his gun back. "I'll get the money to pay you from Mr. Reid today and you can be on your way."

"Thank you, Sheriff," Henry said as he slipped the gun back in his holster. "I'm as glad to get out of here as you probably are to see us leave."

Mitch smiled. "Doesn't matter to me. You did me a favor by going after the Hayes gang with me. You can stay as long as you like." The truth was that Mitch was torn—he knew they were trouble and hoped they would decide to leave the same day. At the same time, he had a telegram out in Denver that probably wouldn't be answered before Monday.

Trace grinned. "Good. I'm keeping company with Miss Jewel tonight to repay her for that fine dinner, so I won't be leaving until Monday."

Henry left, promising to return for his money. Trace took a deep breath. "What're you going to do with Mort's share of the posse money?"

"I'm taking care of that."

Trace raised his eyebrows. "I don't think he had no family."

"If that turns out to be the case, I'll split the money between you and Henry."

Trace started to leave, then turned around and came back. "What do you mean you're taking care of it?"

"Mort said he hooked up with you in Denver, so I've sent a telegram to the sheriff to see if he can locate any family there."

Trace relaxed. "Oh. I don't think he's from Denver. By the way, Mitch, I hope you don't mind about Miss Jewel and me."

Mitch shrugged. "Why would I mind?" He started to roll a cigarette from his makings.

Trace scratched his head. "I guess I thought, well, it seems that you and Miss Jewel kind of like each other. But I got the impression you two had a falling out the other day."

Mitch lit his cigarette and inhaled. "What makes you think that?"

Trace dropped his eyes and cocked his head to the side. "Oh, you know, the way a woman acts around a man when she likes him. But last night when we met you while taking a stroll, she didn't seem very comfortable around you."

Mitch crushed the cigarette under his boot heel and got up from his chair. Trace got up as well.

"I need to go visit Mayor Reid and get the money to pay you for your time," he told Trace. "You will be free to leave town in about an hour."

"Is that a threat?"

Mitch shook his head. "Just a suggestion. You told me a few days ago that you had some business to take care of in Tucson, but it could wait. Now I'm giving you permission to leave."

Trace smiled. "Then since Miss Jewel isn't spoken for,"—he leveled his gaze at Mitch—"I think I'll stay around. At least for a few days."

Chapter Fourteen

Mitch went to see Reid and get the money to pay his temporary deputies. Jewel was in the outer office and she looked up briefly and smiled. Reid gestured for Mitch to come into his office.

"What about Mort Keegan?" Reid asked. "Does he have any kinfolk we can send it to?"

"I'm working on it," Mitch replied. "Trace says Mort had no family, but I'm not sure how much he knew about Mort to begin with. I think he's just eager to get Mort's portion of the money."

"Well, Trace is a Pinkerton man, Mitch. He knows his business."

Mitch decided not to tell Reid any more than he already had, not until he got confirmation from Denver on some of his questions.

He took the money and left Reid's office. Jewel was waiting for him in the outer office. "I enjoyed last night with Trace," she said.

Mitch felt his jaw tighten in response. "I'm glad you had a good time." He hoped he didn't sound as if he was choking on the words. He really did hope she had a good time, but he still suspected that Trace was up to no good, and he didn't want Jewel caught in the middle of trouble. "Are you going to that dance with him tonight?"

She stared hard at Mitch without responding right away, then finally said, "Yes. He's taking me to the dance. We're going to have a good time. He is very charming."

Mitch wished her well. Before he took his leave, he said to her, "Jewel, just please be careful."

She looked at Mitch with curiosity. "What do you mean?"

Mitch weighed what he should say to her. "I just don't think he's going to stick around town. Don't get yourself hurt over him."

Instead of thanking him, Jewel gave him a stony look. "How dare you tell me how to live my life. And it's none of your business if I get hurt. At least Trace Beaumont pays attention to me!" She quickly turned her back on Mitch and furiously sorted through some papers. She stopped and turned back to face Mitch. "And for your information, I have no designs on Mr. Beaumont. If he left town tonight, I wouldn't care a fig."

Mitch left the office and went in search of Trace and Henry.

He found the two men at the hotel where they were staying and paid them for their services. Although Trace was no longer wearing the sling, he moved as if his shoulder still gave him some pain.

151

"I can take Mort's money," Trace offered. "Maybe I was wrong about him not having a family. Since I work for Pinkerton, maybe I can check into it. There has to be someone who deserves what Mort earned."

Mitch smiled. "That's all right. I'm looking into it right now. If I don't get an answer, I'll split it between you and Henry if you're still here. If not, it goes to the church building fund."

Trace nodded. "I met the good reverend at breakfast about an hour ago. He told me he's almost got enough money in the bank to start building his house of worship."

That was a lot of money, Mitch knew. The reverend had been saving up for not only the building, but stained glass windows, which were expensive, and a bell to call his worshipers to the service.

Mitch worried about the look in Trace's eyes when he mentioned it.

Saturday night came much too quickly and was more of the same as Friday night—drunk miners staggering from saloon to saloon, loud laughter and hearty singing accompanying slightly out-of-tune saloon pianos, bottles and chairs breaking as fights broke out over one drunk miner saying the wrong thing to another miner.

At one end of town, the old livery stable was lighted up with the sound of stomping feet and clapping hands, couples of all ages dancing to the fiddle tunes that were sawed out by rusty musicians. Mitch stopped by a few times, and always stayed outside the doors, just looking in to make sure everything was going well.

The Reverend Mr. Wesslund spied him at one point and Mitch couldn't get away in time to avoid him.

"Sheriff, I hope to see you at the sermon tomorrow morning." The preacher was a short, round little man with bushy muttonchops and balding on top. He wore black pants and a black coat over a starched white shirt and paper collar.

"Reverend," Mitch greeted him. "How goes the church fund?"

"We're almost there, my friend," Wesslund said, clapping Mitch on the back. "This Sunday social may give us enough money to start building that church."

For as long as Mitch had been in Paxton, the preacher had been talking about building a church. And from what J. Paxton Reid had said, Wesslund always had an excuse for not building that church. Mitch wondered if it would ever come to pass. It made no difference to him, but he didn't like to see the good folks of Paxton give money to a fund that would never be put to use.

"I understand that you were in Hayden two days ago."

Wesslund blinked in surprise, then seemed to recover. "Yes, how did you know?"

Mitch explained why he'd been there. Frankly, he was surprised the circuit preacher could afford such an expensive hotel room. Preachers usually found a citizen in town who could give them a bed for the night. He told Wesslund so.

"Er, yes. I stayed one night there. They sometimes have a free room for me."

"Did you happen to see this man?" He described Mort Keegan.

Wesslund thought about it, then shook his head. "He

sounds familiar," the preacher said slowly, "but I'm afraid I can't be more certain than that."

Mitch thanked the preacher and promised to be at the social, then moved on to check the saloons again. Alky was back at the jailhouse, resting his foot and keeping company with the men who had already been escorted to a cell.

At the Bad Dog, Mitch stopped in to make sure no one was cheating at cards. Reid was sitting in on a game, but when he saw Mitch come in, he told the dealer to deal him out of the next few hands. He got up and went over to Mitch.

"Jewel told me you still don't trust Trace Beaumont," Reid said. "Why don't you leave him alone. It's clear that you're a little jealous of the fact that Jewel has turned her attentions to him."

Mitch sighed and took his makings out to roll a cigarette. "Mr. Reid, I have good reason to suspect him, and until I hear back from Denver, I won't let it rest. There's something wrong with Mort Keegan's death."

Reid looked surprised. "But I thought, Trace told me, that the Tucson deputies caught the man. It was the hotel clerk who stole the bank money and killed your deputy."

Mitch lit his cigarette and inhaled. "That's the story, but I've written down everything that happened and it doesn't make sense."

"Tell me."

So Mitch told him about the day clerk taking the bank money out of the safe and handing the packet to him.

"Maybe the night clerk wasn't too smart," Reid said. "Or maybe he was too smart and put the money in the safe on the chance that the murder would be discovered and linked to the money," Mitch replied. "But either way, I don't figure this night clerk to be a killer. Especially not the vicious way Mort Keegan was killed."

Reid agreed with Mitch on that point.

Mitch remembered Tim, the night clerk. The man didn't look as if he would have been able to kill a fly, let alone knife a man. On the other hand, Mitch had no problem seeing Henry or Trace killing Mort.

The idea of Pen and Elmer Hayes putting money in a hotel safe didn't sit right either. Finding a loose floorboard or hiding the money on a rooftop above a certain hotel room would be more likely.

Reid looked troubled. "You sure you're not just tryin' to run down Trace out of jealousy? I know you like my daughter, and you know I don't approve of the friendship you two have."

Mitch shrugged. "Think what you like. But I have my reasons for not trusting everything Trace said."

"I thought Trace saved you from drowning when you were little."

Mitch nodded. "He did. But he was always a sly kid. He was caught in a couple of lies. People don't change that much over time."

Reid pushed off from the bar and said, "You tell me what you learn about him, Mitch. I want to know if my daughter has anything to worry about."

"I will."

Reid went back to his poker game and Mitch went on with his rounds.

Chapter Fifteen

By Sunday morning, the citizens of Paxton were buzzing about the dance the previous night. Excitement charged the very air as men, women, and children gathered to hear the sermon Wesslund was willing to deliver.

Mitch had barely woken in time, splashed his face with water, had a quick cup of coffee boiled from the night before, and an even quicker smoke. The sermon was delivered from the old livery stable where the dance had been held the night before. The smells of old straw and sweat, and the faint tang of lemonade mingled together. Flies hovered crazily above the spots where sweet lemonade had spilled on the floor the night before.

Wesslund was in fine form, reading excerpts from the books of Nehemiah and Ruth, pounding on the homemade pulpit and rumbling about fire and damnation. But it was clear that the crowd was restless and he was wise enough to cut his speech short. Everyone was looking forward to the social.

The families filed out of the livery stable, most of them stopping to greet the preacher before going home to get ready for the social, which would be held in the same place in the early afternoon.

"Sheriff, you are planning on the social, aren't you?" Wesslund asked.

"I'll be back here to make sure everything goes well," Mitch said.

The preacher turned to the man next to Mitch. Mitch recognized him as Ephraim Hawkes, the bank manager.

"Ah, Mr. Hawkes, I have a favor to ask you."

Ephraim was a tall, pale man with a weak handshake who would be more at home as an undertaker than as a banker. He gave Wesslund a ghost of a smile.

"What can I do for you, Reverend?"

"When the social is over, would you be so kind as to escort me to the bank to put the money from the box lunches in my church fund?"

"Well, it is Sunday, the Lord's Day," Ephraim said thoughtfully. He had a nervous way of working his fingers as if he were playing the piano or maybe more appropriately working on an adding machine. "Would I be breaking any church laws by opening for business?"

The preacher chuckled heartily and pumped Ephraim's hand. "It's the Lord's work we're doing, Mr. Hawkes."

"Then, I suppose that would be fine."

Mitch watched the two men leave together, the preacher enthusiastically explaining the kind of church he wanted to see built.

Several men stayed behind to sweep the old stable clean and lay down new straw. Mitch watched all this for a few minutes, but as soon as he decided he wasn't needed there, he started to head back to the jail.

"Mitch!" Jewel called out.

He turned and waited for her to catch up. He could see her father standing with the preacher, watching them over Ellie West's shoulder.

Mitch touched his hat to acknowledge Reid, then turned his attention to Jewel.

"Mitch, I wanted to apologize for being so touchy lately. You didn't do anything to deserve the way I've been treating you."

Mitch nodded. "I appreciate that."

She looked away. "It's just that—you know I like you. I get the feeling it's mutual."

Mitch nodded.

She looked back at him. "My father told me that you suspect Trace of holding something back, some information."

Mitch waited.

"I'm going to find out what it is, Mitch."

He frowned. He knew he couldn't tell her what to do. Jewel was headstrong. If her father couldn't control her, he certainly couldn't either. "Don't do anything to get yourself in trouble, Jewel. I wouldn't want that to happen."

"I promise to be subtle."

They locked eyes for a moment and she smiled. "I have to go fix my box lunch," she finally said. "I'll see you at the social."

They parted ways.

* * *

A few hours later, the social was in full swing. Most people were in a good mood as the box lunches came up for bid. Some had several men bidding furiously on their lunches—Miss Ellie of Ellie's Eat Here café had a lunch that went for twelve dollars.

When Jewel's lunch came up for bid, Trace began the bidding, Mitch followed, and several other men bid on it as well. The other men dropped out after seven dollars, but Mitch and Trace kept it up.

"Mr. Beaumont, do you want to make it seven fifty?" Wesslund asked.

Trace nodded.

The preacher looked at Mitch, who nodded. "That's eight dollars."

Trace locked eyes with Mitch, then raised his hand.

The delighted preacher said, "Eight fifty."

Mitch raised his hand.

"Nine dollars."

Trace called out, "Ten dollars."

"Eleven," Mitch said.

"Twelve," Reid called out.

"Fifteen," Trace said.

The crowd gasped. Jewel caught Mitch's eye and shook her head. He understood and dropped out.

As Trace came up to Wesslund to pick up his lunch and Jewel to share it with him, the crowd clapped. Trace gave a little bow, looking triumphantly over to Mitch.

Mitch touched the brim of his hat to acknowledge Trace's win, then retreated to the back of the room. Jewel glanced over at Mitch and gave him a brief nod.

Someone clapped him on the back. Mitch looked around to find Reid there. "Better luck next time," he said, but it was clear from his expression that he didn't mean it.

It was later that day, close to suppertime, that Reid came into Mitch's office.

"How was the social?" Mitch asked.

"Just fine," Reid said. "Have you seen Jewel?"

"No." Mitch took his makings out and rolled a cigarette. "She's not back from the picnic with Trace?"

"No. She said she'd be back before now. Miss Ellie promised to make a fine dinner for us tonight."

"Maybe time just got away from her."

Reid continued to look troubled, but he nodded. "Maybe."

"I'll go out and check around town. You go home in case she's back by now."

"Sure," Reid said. He turned away, then turned back. "Thanks, Mitch."

Mitch walked around town and asked folks if they'd seen Jewel. No one had seen her since she went on the picnic with Trace. Finally he figured he'd better check in on Reid to see if she'd come back home.

He went over to Reid's house, a large two-story, the only two-story in town, and knocked. Reid answered the door, but didn't open it more than a few inches.

"Yes?"

"I couldn't find Jewel, Mr. Reid."

"Oh. Well, she's back. Thanks for checking on her, though."

Mitch wondered how she had fared with Trace—had she gotten information out of him that Mitch couldn't get? "Can I talk to her?"

Reid looked flustered. "Well, actually, she's making the evening meal right now."

"Oh. Well, I'll talk to her tomorrow."

Reid closed the door. Mitch walked away, very troubled. Reid had told him earlier that Miss Ellie was cooking for the two of them tonight.

Mitch headed over to Miss Ellie's café. Sunday was the only night she closed up, but she was in the back with the supplies, taking inventory. She had a piece of paper propped up on a board and was counting and scribbling numbers down.

"Hello, Sheriff. You know I'm not cooking tonight," Ellie said.

"Hello, Miss Ellie. Mr. Reid told me that you were cooking for him and Jewel tonight."

Ellie smiled. "Yes, we had made plans, but I was told that he sent his regrets and hoped we could plan for dinner next Sunday."

"Did Reid come over and tell you himself?"

She looked flustered and unsure of herself for a moment. "Why, no. As a matter of fact, I thought it was strange, but the reverend came around here himself." She put down her paper and pencil and looked at Mitch. "Is something wrong, Sheriff?"

He didn't want to alarm her, but he wondered what Wesslund had to do with Reid's and Jewel's plans for dinner. It was possible that he was just a messenger, but Mitch didn't like it one bit. Especially the secretive way Reid behaved at the door, as if there were someone behind it holding a gun to his head. Or Jewel's.

"No, Miss Ellie, nothing's wrong. You just go on about your business." He turned and left.

Chapter Sixteen

Mitch crept up the back way to J. Paxton Reid's place. The shades were down in all the windows, but he could hear voices in the parlor. He recognized Reid's voice, and Jewel's. And a third voice, a man's. He couldn't be certain of who it was, but he thought it was someone he knew.

He knew that one of the windows on the second floor didn't have a lock on it. It was in Jewel's room. She'd once told him that she used to sneak out of her room early in the morning to go watch the sunrise or to ride her horse without her overprotective father watching her every move.

He climbed a tree outside the window and shinnied out on a limb until he was near enough to the window to hear if there was anyone in the room. It was quiet.

As silently as he could, he slid the window open and slipped inside. It was dark and cool. He wished he had a light, but he wasn't sure where Jewel kept her matches and kerosene lamps. He didn't want to stumble over anything in her room and give away the fact that he was in the house, so he pulled the curtain back until his eyes adjusted to the dark, helped by a little light from the window. When he had memorized the room, he let the curtain drop back into place so no one would suspect that anything was wrong.

He took his boots off, but kept ahold of them as he crossed the room in stocking feet, stopping every time a board seemed about to give him away with a creak. Within a few minutes, he was at the door that led to the hallway. He opened it slowly, hoping that Jewel or Reid kept it oiled properly, and was rewarded with silence.

"This is preposterous," Reid was saying downstairs. "Let us go this instant."

"You know I can't do that," said a male voice. Trace Beaumont.

"My daughter has nothing to do with this. Leave her alone."

"Ow!" Trace said. "The little bitch bit me." Mitch heard a hand slapping Jewel's face.

"Henry, you keep an eye on these two until I'm finished with our business, then we'll get out of here." There was a pause as the front door opened. "And maybe we'll take Miss Jewel with us for insurance."

The door closed. Mitch slid out of the room during that exchange. He unholstered his gun. He knew he had to be careful because he wasn't sure exactly where Jewel or Reid were seated in the parlor, and he wanted to make sure that he didn't shoot anyone but Henry. He bided his time to make sure there was enough distance between Trace and the house so Trace wouldn't hear the gunshots and come back.

He let a few minutes go by, imagining where Trace was. He figured Trace had overheard Wesslund say he was going to the bank with Ephraim Hawkes. Trace knew that there was a large building fund in the bank, as well as miners' money. He'd missed out on the Tucson bank robbery money when Mitch found it and returned it to the deputies heading back to Tucson, so Trace was robbing the Paxton Bank as a way to make up for it.

When Mitch figured enough time had passed, he crept halfway down the stairs. Henry's back was to him, but Jewel and Reid saw his shadow. Mitch could make out where Reid and Jewel were tied to dining room chairs. Jewel didn't say anything, but her eyes widened.

Mitch tossed his boots the rest of the way down the stairs to distract Henry, who wheeled around, gun in hand, and shot at the empty boots. Mitch threw himself down the remaining stairs as he shot at Henry. Henry shot back, but his aim was wide. He fell to the floor with three bullets in him.

Mitch quickly got up and, gun still in hand, came into the parlor and untied Jewel. She rubbed her wrists, then got up and threw her arms around Mitch. "Thank you."

He gently unwrapped her arms. "Untie your father. I have to put on my boots and go over to the bank."

She nodded and turned to her father.

"Mitch," Reid said. Mitch turned around. "Thank you. They were going to kill us. I know it."

Mitch nodded and got his boots back on. One of

them had a bullet hole in it. Henry had been a good shot, fast and accurate. So had Billy the Kid. But now that he was dead, Mitch would never know if Henry Sturms was really Billy the Kid. But if he had escaped Pat Garrett's bullet that night several years ago in Fort Sumner, New Mexico, he hadn't escaped Mitch's gun. The outlaw, if this was him, was well and truly dead now.

"Do you have a shotgun?" Mitch asked Reid, who was now rubbing his wrists to get the circulation back into them.

Jewel got up and went to the back of the house. She returned with a shotgun and a handful of shells.

"Go tell Alky about the trouble at the bank. Stay off the main street," he told Reid.

"Be careful, Mitch," Reid said.

Mitch left Reid's house and headed for the bank. It was dusk outside, which fact would be to his advantage if Trace had heard the shots.

The bank was located on the north end of town. Mitch crouched low and ran under the large window that faced out onto the street. It was a conceited and impractical addition to the wooden bank, one that the bank owner, J. Paxton Reid, had installed to call attention to Paxton's first bank. Mitch remembered telling Reid that it was foolish to put into a place where people expected their money to be safe. Reid had addressed Mitch's concern by installing black iron bars over the window, which gave the bank a sort of jail-like look, as if the bank were holding everyone's money prisoner. But it didn't seem to stop people from depositing their money in the bank and making it a success.

Now the bank manager, and possibly the preacher,

was probably being held hostage as Trace filled his bags, ready to leave town with everyone's money.

Mitch slid around the corner of the bank and saw two horses saddled and ready to leave town. He positioned himself so he would be waiting when Trace came out. A minute later, Trace walked around the corner, his saddlebags stuffed with money, slung over his left shoulder. His gun was in his right hand.

Mitch stepped out. "So you're not a Pinkerton agent."

Trace stopped and dropped the bags to the ground. He grinned, the gun still at his side. "No. I knew I couldn't fool you, Mitch."

"Drop your gun and come with me."

Trace shook his head. "I'm not going with you, Mitch. You won't take me—" He brought the gun up but Mitch shot first, aimed right at Trace. Mitch's shots hit Trace in the left shoulder and the gut. Blood and bone exploded, a look of pain crossed Trace's face; then he crumpled to the ground.

Mitch dropped the shotgun and went over to kneel by Trace's body. He was dead. The click of a hammer caused him to look up. The good Reverend Mr. Wesslund stood over him, gun in hand.

"You're the fifth member of the Hayes gang," Mitch said.

The preacher wasn't smiling now. "I've come to make a withdrawal. Toss those bags over to me."

Mitch slowly reached toward the saddlebags, then started to pick them up. When Trace had been shot, he dropped his gun, and it had fallen underneath the saddlebags. Mitch reached underneath and grabbed the gun, launching himself sideways as he shot the preacher again and again and again.

Wesslund's body jerked with each shot until he finally fell backward, face upturned to the sky. His eyes were open to heaven.

On Monday morning, Alky came into the office with a piece of paper. "Morning, Sheriff."

"Morning, Alky. What've you got?"

"Telegram. Abner was on his way here and gave it to me to give to you."

"You read it yet?"

Alky sat down. "Uh-huh." He handed the paper to Mitch. It was from the Denver sheriff confirming that Trace was not a Pinkerton agent. But there was a Pinkerton man named Mort Keegan who was down that way.

Mitch knew he'd have to send an answering telegram to let the Denver Pinkerton office know that Mort Keegan had died in the line of duty. And he'd have to send another telegram to Sheriff MacLean in Tucson telling him that unless they had hard evidence against Tim the night hotel clerk as Mort Keegan's killer, it had more likely been Trace, Henry, or Wesslund.

After Mitch had killed Wesslund last night, Reid told him that the circuit preacher had only shown up about two years ago, about when the Hayes gang lost its fifth member.

Jewel Reid entered the office. Both men stood to greet her. Alky offered her the chair and he sat on the corner of the desk.

"How are you doing, Mitch?"

"Just fine, Jewel. How's your father?"

She laughed. "Back at the office as if nothing happened yesterday." Her expression sobered. "Too bad about Trace."

Mitch nodded.

Alky looked at Mitch. "You told me earlier that you didn't like him. He was too silver-tongued. But he saved your life once. What'd he ever do for you to not like him?"

Mitch looked away from Jewel. "He took a girl away from me once."

Jewel blushed. "Mitch, since you missed my fried chicken yesterday, would you like to come over for dinner tonight?"

"I'd like that."

She smiled. "I'd better go tell my father you'll be joining us." She got up and left.

Alky turned to Mitch. "You think Mr. Reid'll ever accept you and Jewel together?"

Mitch shrugged. "We'll see, won't we?"

Alky got up. "I'm gonna get some breakfast. You want to come along?"

Mitch looked up from the telegram. He had to get a reply out soon to free Tim in Hayden. "I'll be along, Alky. Probably no more than ten minutes."

When Alky was gone, Mitch composed the telegrams he had to send. He wrote one to Sheriff MacLean informing him of what went on yesterday, then another to the Denver sheriff's office, informing them of Mort Keegan's death and asking where to send the money Mort had earned as a deputy, and the money he'd get from selling the belongings of one of the outlaws. He wrote the messages on the only free paper he could find—the backs of several wanted posters featuring Billy the Kid that would otherwise have been thrown away.

Then Mitch got up and went over to the general store to have Abner send the messages.

Apache Law

Hellfire

Luke Adams

Mitch Frye has seen a lot of killing in his time. Back when he was one of the Apache scouts with the 6th Cavalry he saw what an Apache could do to an enemy. But he never saw anything like the body he finds in the alley that night. And it isn't long before there are more. It looks like somebody is out to sweep the prostitutes off the streets of Paxton. Somebody who isn't using the law to do the job—but a knife. But cleaning up the town is Frye's job, and now he has a madman to deal with, a butcher who seems dedicated to his bloody work. Mitch knows in his gut that the killing won't stop until he and the killer meet face to face—a meeting only one of them will survive.

___4688-1 $3.99 US/$4.99 CAN

Apache Law

Outlaw Town

Luke Adams

Mitch Frye has only been gone four days. As sheriff of Paxton, he's had to track down a killer and bring him back. Easy enough. But when he tries to ride back into town he finds the trails blocked by gunmen who aren't about to let anyone in . . . or out. And when Frye makes his way into town under cover of night, that's when he sees what's happened—and what he will be up against. An outlaw gang has taken over the town and is holding the leading citizens hostage, demanding that whatever comes out of the local mines goes straight into their own pockets. It is up to Frye to take on the gang single-handedly—one by one or all at once if he has to—with the fate of a whole town hanging in the balance.

___4732-2 $3.99 US/$4.99 CAN

TROUBLE MAN

ED GORMAN

Ray Coyle used to be a gunfighter. And when he gets word his boy has been killed in a gunfight in Coopersville, he has to go there—to bring the body home. But when the old gunfighter steps off the train, he brings his gun with him, along with something else . . . trouble.

___4440-4 $4.99 US/$5.99 CAN

Dorchester Publishing Co., Inc.
P.O. Box 6640
Wayne, PA 19087-8640

Please add $1.75 for shipping and handling for the first book and $.50 for each book thereafter. NY, NYC, and PA residents, please add appropriate sales tax. No cash, stamps, or C.O.D.s. All orders shipped within 6 weeks via postal service book rate. Canadian orders require $2.00 extra postage and must be paid in U.S. dollars through a U.S. banking facility.

Name_____
Address_____
City_____State_____Zip_____
I have enclosed $_____ in payment for the checked book(s).
Payment <u>must</u> accompany all orders. ☐ Please send a free catalog.
     CHECK OUT OUR WEBSITE! www.dorchesterpub.com

WILD BILL

DEAD MAN'S HAND

JUDD COLE

Marshal, gunfighter, stage driver, and scout, Wild Bill Hickok has a legend as big and untamed as the West itself. No man is as good with a gun as Wild Bill, and few men use one as often. From Abilene to Deadwood, his name is known by all—and feared by many. That's why he is hired by Allan Pinkerton's new detective agency to protect an eccentric inventor on a train ride through the worst badlands of the West. With hired thugs out to kill him and angry Sioux out for his scalp, Bill knows he has his work cut out for him. But even if he survives that, he has a still worse danger to face— a jealous Calamity Jane.

___4487-0 $3.99 US/$4.99 CAN

WILD BILL

JUDD COLE

THE KINKAID COUNTY WAR

Wild Bill Hickok is a legend in his own lifetime. Wherever he goes his reputation with a gun precedes him—along with an open bounty of $10,000 for his arrest. But Wild Bill is working for the law when he goes to Kinkaid County, Wyoming. Hundreds of prime longhorn cattle have been poisoned, and Bill is sent by the Pinkerton Agency to get to the bottom of it. He doesn't expect to land smack dab in the middle of an all-out range war, but that's exactly what happens. With the powerful Cattleman's Association on one side and land-grant settlers on the other, Wild Bill knows that before this is over he'll be testing his gun skills to the limit if he hopes to get out alive.

___4529-X $3.99 US/$4.99 CAN

Dorchester Publishing Co., Inc.
P.O. Box 6640
Wayne, PA 19087-8640